Future Bright Light

CATHLEEN ELLIS

OTHER BOOKS BY CATHLEEN ELLIS

www.CathleenEllis.com

A Scarf of Promise	Old Crooked Road
Castle in the Air	Just Let It Go
Making Our Way	Tend My Flowers
Kara's Love	Together Now
Baskets on Christmas Lane	Sky Tossed
Up To Me	A Humble Task
Christmas Bright	What's Beneath
A Voice for Gabby	Loving Presence
Love Ties	Shadow to Sunshine
Roses for Meredith	Carry Me On

1

Before Christmas 2005

"What you wanta do for your 15th birthday?" Jeff asked as they stopped their bikes in the driveway of Audra's home. They parked, locking their bikes. She let them in with her house key.

"Put your stuff in the kitchen. Our housekeeper, Toby, promised to leave some of the oatmeal raisin cookies she baked for us. I'll drop my stuff in my room."

Audra returned from upstairs and set out the cookies on the kitchen island. Jeff already poured milk for them.

"Nuthin', hey, I don't want to do nuthin' for the day, my birthday, just want to celebrate Christmas, like always. What I do want is a second volunteer gig. Mom doesn't want me to work, says she's got it all covered. But she tells me volunteering's OK. Jeffy, I want to make a difference, in people's lives. I feel like I'm spinnin' my wheels, such a conflict for me. Yeah, I have your friendship, and I love you and my family. Somehow, that just's not enough, just not that good for me." She paused, nodding to him, "Music helps."

They dug into their third cookie each as they sat next to each other.

"Dra, let's review what's goin' on in your world. You and me, friends, since, like third grade."

He looked at her, a beautiful face he loved since forever. And her long shining hair, a riot of very dark brown mixed with a reddish hue. But it was her eyes, changing from a medium brown to black with her mood. For him she was a total hottie: tall, slim hips, high breasts, and legs that went on and on. When they stood together, at 5'8" she still had him by an inch.

"My secret hope, someday to be taller than her," he thought.

"I'm waiting, Jeff, I know you're off somewhere, my dear red-haired palfriend."

"Yeah, you're right," he smiled to her, "since your dad's been gone, I'm thinkin' you're pushing yourself really hard."

"Yeah, dad, before Christmas, tumor took him so fast. It wasn't much of a holiday time last year. But I kept hearing him in my head and still do, 'You're my bright light, a light I've always seen, that's within you.' He told me that, from the first that I could ever remember and for all the rest of the time he was in my life."

She put her head in her hands, then raised up and looked Jeff in the eye.

"Maybe that's what happened. You could think only about him, so you basically shut everybody else out of your life."

"Yeah, I know folks asked what they could do to help, me and mom, us just numb and unspeaking. The employees at mom's office, our church, and the girls in my dance class, they tried."

She watched him shake his head, a sadness suddenly pulling his lips in a thin line.

Audra felt her tears start as she gazed at him.

"Uh huh, I needed to grieve; mom's folks came in the new year, to especially comfort mom and me. My granddad finally got time off. You know how crazy the post office is at the holidays. You met them, didn't you?"

"Yeah, you invited me over. You had a few days to recover from the emotions of the celebration of your dad's life. Wow, was I ever surprised. I've never met Eskimo folks before. But I now understand the exotic look of your mom."

"Uh, both my grandparents are tall and hugely handsome, their bronze skin, with that black, black hair, that's still dark, and their so dark, so different eyes, Inuit."

"That's another name for Eskimo?"

"Right."

"For sure your mom picked all that up from them. But, Dra, you also got some of your dad, the very tall dude. His genes really lightened up your skin, your hair, but not your eyes. They turn black when you're really torked off. And you've got your dad's round eyes."

"Yeah, a blue-eyed blonde will do that to you," she smiled as she nodded to Jeff, "genetics," as she pulled on strands of her hair and pointed to her eyes.

"So I'm helping out around home now; doing laundry, keeping up my bedroom and cleaning two bathrooms, making dinner on the days the housekeeper isn't here to cook. It makes me feel good, useful, besides the constant studying. This summer I'm asking mom if I can do the outside mowing and stuff, watering and all that. I gotta start making a difference, at home too, like I said a little while ago."

"Uh, start lookin' at schools; my folks, already pushin' me. My big sis, she's a tough act I can never follow."

"Heck, Jeffy, you're you, a different person from her. Hope your folks will lighten up."

"Maybe, hey how did your PSAT's come out?"

"Good, not sure if I scored high enough for National Merit Scholarship qualifying." She shook her head, "The stats, whew, of the 1.5 million who take the PSAT, about 8 thousand qualify for scholarships."

"Scary stat for you, but your family, you'll be OK. Well that sure as heck is not gonna be my situation. My PSAT're, just decent."

He turned to her, shaking his head and downing the last of his milk.

"HOPE, right?"

"That's it; Georgia tries to take care of its kids who want college. I just wish more kids could take advantage of it."

"The deal is."

"Yeah, Dra, the deal is you gotta work, make grades, prove you can do the work in high school, and every semester after that, at the university level. And you and me, we, we've talked about the war, about all the girls in Iraq and Afghanistan, lots of them can't even go to school. You're so lucky to live in America."

Audra nodded to him, "Yeah, I think about that too, Jeff, about if I'd been born in one of those countries. So, I know an education is a gift, it really is. I'll do the work, get my education, for me, but also for all those girls who won't be able to."

"Yeah, I guess it's better for guys in those countries. Hey, I gotta stay in state, for the HOPE, but there're plenty of schools. I just gotta figure out what I want to do."

"Well, I'm serious about helpin' folks, so teaching or nursing, that'd be me. I know those're the old standards, but that's me. Dad's an alum of Auburn. They got a nursing school there, so that's a possibility. That bright light, that my dad always called me, I know he wants me to have a special meaning for my life, to make a difference, yeah. My heart says that's what he wants for me."

"Hey, he's still such an important part of your life," Jeff paused and gazed at her, "your mom, where's she from?"

"Alum of the University of Alaska."

"So far away."

"Yeah, mom was born in Nome, Alaska. Granddad Tsosie got a promotion to a regional office of the US Postal Service, from Nome to Helena, Montana, when Mom was 10. So she grew up in way super cold, never forgot that experience. Going to school in Anchorage, at the U of A, that did it for her, a remembrance of the snow, of her early days. But then her whole life changed when she got admitted to law school, at University of Virginia Law."

"She exchanged cold for extreme heat and humidity."

"Well she never said, uh, mom's not a complainer. She's kept losing dad pretty much to herself."

"Counseling?"

"Some, but, bein' a lawyer, well she doesn't take advice very well; she's used to dishing it out. And she's way busier now, taking over some of dad's clients. Her solace is church on Sunday, our quiet day; she loves that, going with me, her day with God."

"I gotta take off. Make those times with your mom, make them special, Audra. I try to live for just today, 'cause."

She felt his clear blue eyes pierce her dark brown ones.

She nodded, "I know Jeffy, yesterday's gone and tomorrow's, well we can't see ahead."

"Right, hey, before I leave, let's do one of our songs."

"Yeah, it'll make me feel better, you know, before dad died, well," she paused, "we did some Bible reading. Dad, he wanted to be with me."

"Uh huh, you told me, the psalm about singing praises to God?"

"That's right, besides to God I always lift up my songs to dad, he rides upon the clouds. That's how I visualize him."

"Right, every time you look up into the sky?"

She nodded to Jeff.

Audra sat down at the grand piano and played the chord they needed. Jeff sang out, in his tenor, harmonizing her alto voice. They listened to each other sing.

"His voice, it's made an awesome change, a so cool switch from his boy soprano to his young man tenor," she thought after they finished the piece.

They both participated in an a cappella group of guys and girls, a group begun three years ago by the talented choral director at their Georgia high school, Ephrine High. From middle school on they heard about the fine choral groups at the high school. Audra and Jeff auditioned as freshmen and sang in the group since then.

They hugged. She watched him unlock his bike as she opened the garage door to put her bike in.

"Hey, kid, next year, we're 16, the car in there, for you, right?"

"Yeah, Jeffy, it'll be. Mom and I already talked."

"See ya, hey Happy Christmas."

"Yeah, see ya, to you also, Merry Christmas."

They smiled to each other as she watched him ride away. He turned and waved. She waved back to him.

"My home, it's so beautiful," she spoke out as she walked from the entrance foyer and looked around at the very large living room. "And it's simple, dark wood furniture to match the medium dark wood floor."

Her mom let her decorate the tree, from start to finish. This year they decided on all white lights, different from years past. She drew in a deep breath, taking in the scotch pine smell that permeated the entire first floor of the Davisson home. Audra asked for a tree just a little over six feet, so she could manage stringing the lights by herself. Last year, after her dad died, she and her mom decided not to do a tree, but they made each other a promise.

"Next Christmas, Audra, we'll do a tree of your choice, in the great room, set near the grand piano. How does that sound?"

"Awesome, Mom."

Audra recalled that time, "We hurt so bad, sometimes angry, sometimes sad, at what happened."

She stood in front of the twinkling tree.

"It was all stuff beyond our control, but I know God, I know You had a hand in helping us recover. I am grateful."

She started to sing, in her low alto, "Sweet peace of God, come over me, like a gift from heaven, sweet peace."

She hummed a bit more, then stopped. Audra took the steps to the second floor at her usual two-steps-at-a-time pace. She sat with her calendar and patted the packet of songs on her desk.

She nodded as she spoke out, "We'll surprise the congregation, for Christmas this year, singers. We been practicing singing in rounds. We're small, but mighty. And we been workin' on our songs, like since September."

She recalled last summer when she went to her minister and asked about starting a singing group of 4th-7th graders in the congregation. What surprised her was the interest of the young people who showed up a half hour before service that first Sunday morning.

"Hey, you all, this is a special way to worship God," she smiled to them as the group assembled. "And, you're gonna find," she paused, "that there's a power of music that brings people together. You'll see that when I encourage the congregation to join us, especially at the holidays, when everyone'll know the songs."

She gave them nametags with pin backs to wear until she got to know all of them. The number varied a little, depending on the Sunday, but there were six strong soprano voices and two alto voices among the singers. With Audra it made three alto voices. She sang right along with them. They practiced in a dressing room where the choir kept their outfits. It happened that an old upright piano stayed in the room. Audra used that to give the singers their notes, one melody note for sopranos and a harmony note for the altos.

"You're doin' real good, singers, and you fellas, it's great to have your voices," she nodded and smiled to them after the first time they performed in late fall, the start of Advent. "I especially appreciate your memorizing the notes and the words so quick. You all are super sharp."

She drifted back from her reverie, got up from her desk and looked down at the packet of songs she would take back to church.

"We're ready for Christmas Eve," she nodded.

She went to the kitchen and read the weekly list for the rest of the week, with Christmas on Sunday. For years now her parents and the nanny, now a housekeeper, set up a weekly list of events, foods for meals, and Audra's many activities. A whole year well-worn calendar by month propped up next to the wall phone. Her parents worked long days about twice a week. The calendar kept the family organized.

"Mom, now that it's just you, me and Toby, the calendar's easy. I just got dance Saturday mornings and the half hour before church time for my choir on Sunday. I'm letting the dance go after this semester."

Tonight Audra planned to fix hamburgers and oven-baked fries for her mom and her.

Her mom got home at 4 p.m., early for her. She let her staff go earlier than that. And she gave them Monday off; Sunday was Christmas.

"Packages for you to wrap, are you up for that, Audra?"

"Yup, just get me the stuff to wrap, happy to help. Then I'll start dinner."

Her mom gave her a hug and stepped back away from her, "Sweet Dra, I gotta share how much I appreciate everything you do to help out. You continue to amaze me with all the household stuff you've taken over. After the first of the year I'm just having Toby come in to clean one day and cook for two evening meals a week. She's taking on another housekeeping job. You're doing the laundry and so much cooking. Most of what I need to do is to drive you around Saturdays and Sundays. What'cha think?"

"Mom, hey, I'm so happy to help out. Dad appreciates it; I talk to him a lot, he answers with vibes that let me know."

"That happens to me, especially at work, when I have a tough decision to make, he's sending me advice from his new home."

Ashley stood in front of her daughter, "Anybody listening to this conversation might think we'd lost our noodles," she giggled.

Audra joined in with the laughing, "Uh huh, you just gotta lose someone important."

Ashley gave her daughter eye contact, "Exactly, only then do you understand."

Her mom brought out the boxes that need wrapping. Audra found the container of wrapping paper, bows, and to/from tags in the guest bedroom closet. She got everything out, carried the boxes for wrapping to the guest bedroom, and proceeded with the wrapping.

"I'm helping, that makes me feel good," she blew out a breath.

In two trips she brought the wrapped gifts down to her mom for her to sign her name on the to/from cards. She set them on the counter and started dinner.

They ate, sitting at the large island in the kitchen. Audra couldn't remember the last time they used the elegant dining room table. With the meal nearly finished Ashley put her fork down and brought her napkin to her eyes.

"Your Granddad Clint and Grandma Brenda," she stopped and burst into tears.

"Mom, are you OK?"

"Gotta spit this out," she looked at Audra, "before it gives me a worse ache in my gut."

Audra remained silent as her mom continued to cry. As she settled down she started to talk again, this time Audra heard her breathy tones.

"Sweet Dra, remember when your dad's folks came and stayed for the morning after dad's celebration?"

"Yeah, I do."

"So much going on in their lives."

"Mom, what happened that day; why are you so sad and crying?"

"I asked your grandparents if there were any of Will's things that they might want, in remembrance of him."

Then her mom stopped and shook her head, tears flowing again.

"Only two things, I remember his mom and dad looking at each other and then at me and her saying, the frame with his diploma from Auburn, and the frame with his law degree from the University of Virginia Law. Everything else, absolutely not in our family's taste, foreign to us, this whole house."

Ashley stopped and put her hand to her forehead.

She looked at Audra, "It was the way she said it, her tone of voice, she spat the words out. I felt it then as I had pretty much all along in our marriage, at least. Your Grandma Brenda really dislikes me, big time."

"I'm so sorry, Mom."

Audra went and put her arms around her mom as she sat at the counter crying.

She blew out a breath, "Tomorrow's gonna be hard on you, Mom, for sure. I'll help as much as I can."

"Yeah, I can see it," she thought to herself, "Mom wasn't the beautiful blue-eyed blonde young lady that dad dated all through high school and a little at Auburn."

She spoke out, "Mom, let me know what I can do. The caterers already called, wondering when to deliver the Christmas meal. I told them the time Grandma Brenda wanted. It's outa our hands. Dad's mom, she'll have her way with the meal, and everything connected with their coming here to visit. She orchestrates everything, like going to our church for Christmas Eve and to hear my kid's choir."

"The reason they're coming, Audra, is to be with you. They really really love you, sweetie. Be with them as much as you can, 'cause they have to head back to Montgomery early Monday morning. Your Granddad Clint has court Tuesday morning."

"And it's a super long drive back."

"Seems they don't think anything of it."

"I need to be grateful that they're coming to see me, to see us."

Ashley touched her daughter's cheek, "That's right, to see you and me."

"And in the summer?"

"Yeah, sweet girl, you get to spend a week with Grandpa and Grandma Tsosie in Helena."

They finished their meal. Audra brought out the oatmeal raisin cookies. She poured decaf coffee for her mom and her.

"I love my time with your folks, Mom. They, well, truly are awesome, so many stories they have to tell me, of their early days, of Nome."

"They live in a completely different world from your dad's folks."

"Let's see," Audra began the scenario she knew, "the prominent Montgomery lawyer, from a prominent law firm, at the state capitol, working with the rising stars of Alabama government. The wife, a prominent socialite, of a famous Confederate family, always by the lawyer's side, her with her many volunteer efforts to promote literacy and the arts, the two of them living in luxury. And my dad, sick to death of all the prominence, got out of there, caught up in a college fraternity at Auburn, but still making grades. Finally got free of his tangled web of a family when he left Alabama for law school at the U. of Virginia."

"Hey, you've got that absolutely correct. And then he met me." Ashley nodded her head and gave her daughter a wide smile. "And so we settled in a smaller community, wanting to do good, to serve the public. It was magic for your dad and me, our relationship, what we had together. And you, my dear, the best, the best that ever happened to your dad and me, you're the best."

Audra stood before her mom, "That magic, you and dad, I still think you've got that magic, now, by yourself Mom, and I don't want it ever to leave you."

They hugged, then cleaned up the kitchen and put the dishes in the dishwasher.

"Mom?"

"Yeah, Dra?"

"I think that's the most I've heard you say, in months and months, thank you for sharing with me."

Ashley gathered her daughter in her arms again and held her for a long time.

ॐ

She looked from left to right at her kid's choir. They stood together in the choir room.

"You," she moved her hand from left to right, "you're my best Christmas present, the beauty of your voices, praising God."

They watched her wide smile and nod to them.

"We'll sing our best," a 4th grader burst out, as the choir started to file out to the sanctuary.

They giggled and then got quiet, their church quiet. After their singing they sat together in a reserved front pew of the church with Audra. Most times when they sang they returned to their parents, but this eve the packed church wouldn't allow it. Audra felt a special peace come over her, after they all sang and through the service, and all the next day, Christmas, Christ's birth.

"Judge not, judge not," Audra kept telling herself as the time neared for her grandparents to depart.

Her granddad asked to talk with her away from her mom and grandma. They stood together on the far side of the grand piano.

He spoke in his soft quiet Southern drawl, "Wanted to check in with you, any more bullying, or sneerings about your origin?"

"Not," she smiled as she looked into her granddad's dark blue eyes.

"That's good, you know what to do, if it ever happens again."

"I do; I feel certain it won't happen again, word got around fast. And Granddad, I always remember your suggestion, to stay away."

"From the booze and the drugs, huge problems for young people, like what I've talked to you about, the folks who come into my courtroom," he nodded his head to her.

"You are so correct; I've seen so much trouble, with kids at school, awful."

He touched her shoulder as he looked into her very dark eyes.

"Audra," he paused, " you're a gift from God. I know you understand that. And I'm a gift from God, as we all are. Sometimes we lose sight of that. God loves you, and so do I."

"I love you, Granddad."

They hugged. Audra went to her Grandma Brenda to especially thank her for the little birthday cake she presented to Audra at the Christmas dinner.

"The day of your birth, a very special day, in our lives, Audra," her grandma smiled to her.

Once her grandparents left for their long drive home Audra helped clean up the kitchen from the early breakfast of coffee and donuts. She went to the grand piano to play the same song her grandma asked her to play before they left. As she played from memory her mind drifted to the start of her freshman year, when she auditioned for the a cappella group. After she learned she got a slot in the group a very angry girl approached her at her locker.

Audra knew her from middle school. The girl moved closer and closer to Audra, pinning her against her own locker. The girl's bright red face and bulging eyes scared Audra.

"Half breed, go back to Eskimo land. I deserve to be in the choir; I definitely sing better than you," the girl hissed.

Audra attempted to move from her locker. The girl pinned her against the locker again. A passing student stopped and told the girl to get away. She slowly moved from Audra.

The boy shook his head to Audra, "That crud, not allowed at school, no bullying here."

He eyed the bully, "Let's go, bully, you, to the office. I'm reporting this."

After a meeting with the principal, the girl, the girl's parents, and Audra's parents with Audra present, the bullying stopped. The girl's parents took her to anger management classes. And a school counselor kept an eye on her. Jeff encouraged Audra to continue in the a cappella group. She did so, but the fear of attack took a long time to leave her.

Audra finished the song at the piano, "Thank you God, for taking care of me, and for the boy standing up for me."

She nearly forgot about the whole incident, until her granddad brought it up. "He's a kind and concerned man, my Granddad Clint is," she spoke out.

Audra found her mom in her bedroom, propped up against pillows, her eyes half closed. She held papers in one hand.

"Come in, sweet Dra, I'm just thinkin' about this project at work. To let you know, with the work load, I've decided to bring on a paralegal, instead of another lawyer, at least for awhile. It's all about the money."

Audra sat down next to her mom's legs.

"That's so good, Mom, you don't need more stress in your life, so having help with the workload," she nodded.

Ashley leaned forward and touched Audra's cheek, "Hey, young lady, you are super sensitive to what you need, and to what I need. You've grown up so much, in the last few months. This is a special time of your life, and I want you to enjoy these next years of high school, precious years."

Audra gave her mom a wide smile and nodded, "Precious."

"When you feel up to it, there're two drawers in the low chest in the closet, dad's things. Go through it, if stuff you want, take it. Otherwise, we'll give away, along with the chest. I just don't have time, or the energy, right now."

"Happy to help, Mom, those are the kinds of chores I like, sorta an adventure."

ℂ

On Tuesday morning Ashley went back to work. Before she headed out she stopped by Audra's room. She peeked in.

"Morning sunshine, can I come in?"

"I'm awake, Mom, just saying my prayers and talking to dad."

"It'll be long days at work for the rest of the week, then another three day weekend for me and my staff. Wanta do a hike, maybe New Year's Day morning, after early church?"

"That sounds great, I know Toby's off this week, so I'll fix dinners you've planned, and get the housework and laundry all caught up, plus I got books to read."

"You know how much I appreciate that; a couple of nights we'll eat out."

After her exercise routine and dance practice on the rug in the basement Audra showered and headed to the kitchen.

"Good, thanks mom, you left me enough coffee."

She sipped the hot brew and popped two waffles in the toaster. She had the half of the orange her mom saved for her.

"Time for me to check out dad's stuff."

Audra stepped into her mom's bedroom. It wasn't the same room she remembered when her dad lived.

"Mom replaced the king bed with just a full size." She paused as she touched the lovely light lavender bedspread. "The bedspread, it matches the curtains mom's got now, such a complete change."

She remembered her mom repainting the room one weekend after Valentine's Day last year, doing a lot of crying as she did so.

"The pale blue room, it helped calm mom through those first few rough months, missing dad, I'm sure of that," she spoke out.

"Oh my gosh, dad, all your stuff."

Audra stood there. One whole side of the walk-in closet was completely empty. She saw; nothing remained of her dad's clothes, ties, belts and shoes.

"When did mom have time to do all this?"

"Look through the small set of drawers, dad's things," she remembered her mom saying. "Take what you want."

Kneeling in front of the drawers in the closet, Audra opened the top one, and seeing a black box, she eased it out of the drawer. It looked kind of like a small jewelry box, like a place to put cuff links. She dropped the heavy box on the rug. The lid came off and everything spilled out. The drop caused the red velvet cushioning on the inside of the top of the box to fall out. She saw several small items that did not come out when the cushioning fell. She dislodged the two items from the lid top and placed them in the palm of her hand.

"Hhhmmm, Greek letters on the pin, gosh it's pinned to the gold link on the other pin, and another set of letters. Gosh, dad, how'd these guys get here?"

She set the two attached pins aside and went through the rest of her dad's box. There were cuff links, tie clasps, several tie pins, and a pin that said National Honor Society.

"Hey, the NHS pin looks like ones I've seen. I didn't know you were in that group in high school, dad. There's tons I don't know about you."

She put all the jewelry and the box together, for a thrift shop. She looked through the bottom drawer and found several bow ties, and handkerchiefs that were never used. Audra bagged everything up so she could let her mom know what she intended to do with the stuff. There was now an empty set of drawers that her mom could use or give away.

"I'm not going to show mom these two pins, 'cause somethin' is not quite correct about one of them."

She took a small plastic bag and cut it down to size, just big enough to put the pins in. When she got back to her room, she sat the bag down and moved her books for reading to one side of her desk. Audra turned on her rose-colored reading lamp and took another look at the pins.

"Right, I know that dad joined a fraternity at Auburn."

She looked the pin over and undid the clasp on the back. That freed up the other pin with the chain and attached greek letters. She looked at that pin and turned it over.

"Oh my gosh, there's writing on the back of this pin."

She held it up close to her lamp and read the very tiny inscription, MADALYN SOMNER, on one side of the pin and the tiny numbers 11-02-81 on the other side of the pin. She set the pin down on the desk and patted the pin and the other pin that she thought might belong to her dad. She put the pins back in the tiny bag. The name and the date fried into her brain. A cramp hit her in her stomach and beads of sweat slammed her forehead.

Audra spoke out, "Mom, she wasn't in a sorority, like dad. Besides, she was so far away from him. Who is this Madalyn, and how did her pin get with dad's, oh holy crud, and placed where it was, inside the lining of the box?"

She put the tiny bag she fixed for the pins in her safe place, a small gold oval box. In that box were items she cherished, a small gold bracelet with her name on it. She still could get it around her wrist. It was a baby gift from her Montana grandparents, as was the gold oval box. Next she felt the smoothness of the small pearl stud earrings from her Alabama grandparents. And finally she took out the tiny locket on a gold chain. She opened it to see her dad's tiny picture, just of his smiling face. From time to time she got out the items to look over and wear. Audra didn't care much about clothes, or shoes, or makeup. Her Grandma Brenda bought almost all her clothes and shoes. Audra often heard her say how much she loved doing that for her granddaughter. She just accepted the gesture and wore them all, glad she had such nice things.

Audra treasured her oval box from her Grandpa and Grandma Tsosie. She kept it with her precious items in the back part of the bottom drawer of her small chest of drawers.

"I gotta do some research, and I know who I need to talk to," she told herself.

℘

Audra descended the mountain a little ahead of her mom. She gazed up at the pale blue sky and felt a wind feather her face.

"A wonderful time to be out," she heard her mom's happy voice, "wish I could be out here forever, on this grand New Year's Day."

Audra turned and smiled back to her mom, "But, but, what about all the folks who need your legal expertise."

Ashley pointed to her daughter, "Oh yeah, my clients, it was good to forget about all the stuff going on, for a little while."

On the drive back to Ephrine, mom and daughter talked about Audra's spring semester. They agreed it was time for her to let go of the dance class after the mid-January presentation. Ashley suggested maybe she might like to take a few more voice lessons.

"Mom, I want to try out for the plays Ephrine High does. The drama and choral teachers do, just such an awesome job."

"I can tell you why that is."

"Why?"

"Humphrey University, and Hillyer Academy, they both have programs, and the teachers at Ephrine High, they want that for all of you students."

Audra remembered that both a private university and a private K-12 school also existed in their community.

"Yeah, Mom, that really helps us, everybody is looking for excellence in musical programs."

"Audra, what about your friendships with Isabella and Sophia?"

"Uh huh, you're wondering about that. They both go to Hillyer, so when I leave dance I won't get to see them, unless I plan some times together with them."

"It would be nice." She reached over and touched Audra's shoulder, "I know, I know, Jeff is your very best friend, but you two are really growing up. Your hormones, sex, wanting to be with a special guy or girl, that kinda stuff will start to crop up with him."

"I know, Mom." Audra turned to her mom in the car, "Jeff and me I mean I, yeah, we've talked about this, about how our feelings are changing. He's referred to me as a hottie, a couple of times. I'm gonna ask him to stop that. It's what he sees from his eyes. And what I see from mine, in him, is a super smart red-headed funny guy who I've loved forever."

"You're lucky to have a guy friend like that. But he'll want to date others one day."

"Yeah, I've told him I want him to date; he's reluctant, 'cause we have a really comfortable, really long-term friendship. Right now he just wants to spend time with me, when he's not doing his sports and all his other stuff."

"And once you both start driving, next year, lots will change."

Ashley turned her gaze to her daughter and touched her shoulder.

"I want you to open your heart, as you do to me, and to Jeff, open your heart to others, open it with love."

Audra tracked back through what her mom just said and stayed silent as it sunk in.

"Open with love," she spoke out.

Audra noticed that they approached Ephrine. It was time, she decided.

"Mom."

"Yes, Dra?"

"You're carrying the whole load, Mom, your lawyer work, me, the house, our future. I feel so bad sometimes when I think about that. It's too much, Mom. Sometimes I see the strain in your face, and it makes me sad. I know dad's watchin' out for us, helping, in his way, to maintain what we've got."

"Hey, it's not that bad. We gotta talk about the life insurance of your dad's."

"Mom, you don't want me workin'; you say we're covered. Please tell me that's so."

"Before school starts again, I'll try to sit down with you to show you some numbers, to help you feel better. I'm the adult, let me handle this."

ട്ര

"It's gonna be a busy semester, Audra," Jeff said as they walked to their choral class together.

"Yeah, school work plus I'm trying out for the spring play. I also see the Activities Director at Great Oaks soon."

"You really gonna try to start a Saturday singing group there?"

"I am, seniors love to sing. I have a book of songs they'll know; yeah I've learned a bit about the kinds of music they like. It'll be a super blast and give me a chance to spend time with older folks. They got so much wisdom, to hand down to us."

"Yeah, if we'd just listen," Jeff said as he opened the door for her into the choral room.

"Guy, you are just so smart, golly, I'll remember that pearl of wisdom."

They smiled to each other as they separated and found their chairs in the a cappella choir.

ട്ര

"How's school, Audra?"

"Lovin' it, busy, my science and math classes, the best. And, of course, a cappella, singing, just awesome. I've about decided on a school. But Miss Chamberlain, I really, really need your advice. I'm not sure what I'm walking into, and I absolutely cannot talk to my mom about this, afraid I've stumbled into something," she paused, "well."

Audra stopped and took out the two pins that started causing her some worry and sleeplessness. She laid them on the table between where she and Miss Chamberlain sat.

"Does this stuff have any kind of meaning to you; my dad had a fraternity affiliation while he attended Auburn."

Celia Chamberlain looked the items over, both front and back. She smiled to Audra and nodded her head.

"Absolutely, this possibly was your dad's fraternity pin."

She held it in her hand.

"This may be something of his that you might want to keep, Audra."

"Right, thanks for that idea. Mom asked me to clean out some drawers of his, and to keep or toss stuff. And the other pin with the chain and attached Greek letters?"

"Yes, I was Greek, at the University of Alabama. And this is a sorority pin from a particular sorority, and the attached Greek letters signify the chapter of the sorority. Did you know that there is a name and date on the back of the pin?"

"I did, and that's why I'm here. I'm afraid I may have uncovered something I shouldn't have."

"Go ahead, Audra, I can tell you're upset."

"Please, I need a tissue."

Audra wiped her tearing eyes and her nose that started to drip.

"My," she paused, "my mom, Ashley Tsosie, now Davisson, graduated from the University of Alaska. She wasn't in a sorority. So there is a name on the back of the pin, MADALYN SOMNER and the numbers, a particular date. "Why," she paused as she teared up again, "why did I find my dad's fraternity pin attached to that pin?"

"Wow, Audra, let's have you start from the beginning."

Audra went on to explain how she discovered the pins, that she dropped the heavy box and the lining of the box lid fell out, and how she pulled the pins from inside the lining.

"I honestly think," she shook her head to Miss Chamberlain, "that these were hidden, why?"

"Let's go with what we know. This sorority pin belonged to a Madalyn. By the way that you described to me how you found the pin, uh, attached to the other pin, I would say that this Madalyn and your dad were pinned. That's fancy talk for being pre-engaged. It happens when a couple is not ready to be engaged, still being in school; so this is a way for a couple who love each other to visibly share their love, until they decide the next step. The women wear their sorority pins a lot. Gosh, there's a whole ceremony that goes with this, at the woman's sorority house."

"Sounds like you've seen this."

"I have, several times, so romantic, darkened room, candles, lots of singing of special sorority and fraternity songs."

"Wow, that sounds like a special way for a couple to show they care."

"Exactly."

"I don't know what to do with the pin; I don't want to throw it away."

"Here's where I can help, Audra. My sorority, and all sororities, have national headquarters, where data is kept on all women who've ever been a part of that particular group. I will contact this national headquarters and ask their advice, what to do with the pin. I won't give specifics, just wanting advice. The thing is, Audra, I know you're just a teen, but a college sorority is for life, for all of a woman's life. It's quite precious, the pin, having it get lost can be a tragedy to the woman. That's if it's been lost."

"I wish dad was still alive, maybe he could answer my concerns, this whole pin thing is driving me flippin' crazy. Anyhow my grandparents, my dad's folks, said he dated in college. And he was extremely handsome, so this kinda makes sense, but to hide the pins, I don't get that."

"Everything we've shared, it's confidential, between you and me. Right now your mom, well and you, are still grieving your dad's death. So let's take this one day at a time. I'll let you know what I find out. I know you want to do the correct thing."

Audra got up after she put her precious cargo in a compartment of her backpack.

"I'll get these pins home and in their safe place. Thank you, Miss Chamberlain, I'm starting to feel a little better about my discovery."

Audra stepped forward and hugged her counselor.

As she walked out of the office and closed the door she whispered, "God, help me."

2

"God, you've helped me, thank you," Audra smiled as she walked down the hall, after leaving her counselor's office.

As promised, Miss Chamberlain got back to Audra, just two days later.

"So I did e-mail with the national headquarters of this sorority. They advise to return the pin back to national since the finder (that's you) has no knowledge of the owner of the pin."

She handed Audra a copy of the e-mail with the address of the national headquarters.

"Wow, Miss Chamberlain, as soon as I can I'll get this in a proper package with a note, and send it off. Riding my bike makes errands like this easy for me."

"Thanks for taking care of this. Who knows, the pin may find its way back to its owner."

Audra nodded to her counselor, "That'd be my hope, for sure."

As she stood in front of her locker she decided it was the right thing to do, even though little might ever come of her actions. She rode her bike home from school that day. She realized just how popular her dad once was, based on what her Davisson grandparents told her.

"He was a keeper for my mom," Audra smiled as she thought of her parents together, and apart.

ॐ

Audra peered through the rainy fog as she walked at a brisk pace to Great Oaks. It was only eight blocks from her home, and she had time. She and her mom would eat later that particular evening because she knew her mom had a packed afternoon and early evening at work.

"Thank you for seeing me, Mrs. Lancaster, I watched as you helped folks in the crafts room."

"And thank you for coming by. I read your note about your interest in working with our family (that's what we call ourselves) in a musical effort. I've heard your kid's choir, when I visited your church with a friend. I've no doubt that you have the ability to get seniors to sing out also."

"Thanks, what do you think about the time, Saturday afternoons for 30 minutes, after they have lunch?"

"That sounds wonderful; once word gets out, I think folks will come to sing. You play piano, right?"

"Yes I do, and I stopped by the piano in the large dining room. I played a few chords. It's in pretty good tune."

Mrs. Lancaster laughed, "Ah, yes, we had the darn thing tuned recently because it sounded pretty terrible. However, no one's wanted to play."

She gave Audra a smile, "I can tell you, though, that we have some folks who know piano, and some folks who love to sing. They lack motivation.

You, my dear, are just the motivation they need. You gave me five song ideas in your note. Those are absolutely songs my seniors enjoy, stuff they grew up with."

"Danced to, romanced to, lots of memories."

"That's right, Audra. Tell me about your commitment; I'm interested in a volunteer who's willing to commit for a year. My folks get disappointed easily, so losing you after a few weeks, well, it's kinda hard on them, when they've started looking forward to seeing you. Do you have grandparents?"

"Yes, both in Montgomery, Alabama, and both in Helena, Montana."

"Do you see them on a regular basis?"

"I do, after my dad died a year ago before Christmas, I was able to see all of my grandparents by the new year. Then my Alabama grandparents had Christmas this year with my mom and me. I really appreciate the wisdom of older folks; plus, at least mine, have plain old common sense."

"When would you like to start your singing effort with us?"

"Early February, we'll do a couple of romance songs. I've taken dance for years. In January our dance school does their yearly presentations before the whole community. After that I'm leaving dance. I want to be more involved in drama, both at the high school level, and with community theater. So I'm auditioning for a part in our spring play for our high school. But that won't take away from what I want to do with your family here."

"That sounds very exciting, good luck with that, and yes, I'll call you to let you know our start date, Saturday afternoons in February. I know you'll occasionally need to be away."

"I'll do my best to find someone in the interested group who could play the piano and carry along without me. I'm a junior next year."

"So we'll lose you one day; we all have to move on. Thanks, ahead of time for considering to offer us a volunteer effort. Who knows where this will take all of us."

"It'll be fun and give your family a chance to sing, uh, I hope, joyful time for each of them, thank you," Audra stood and extended her hand to Mrs. Lancaster.

"There are angels among us, dear girl, and you're one of them."

They shook hands as Mrs. Lancaster gave Audra her broad smile.

ℰↄ

"I'm so glad you had a chance to see our dance groups perform, Jeff," Audra said as they headed for their bikes after that school day in early February.

"I wouldn't've missed it. You got some remembrance of it?"

"Uh huh, like in my head and through my legs forever, and a DVD, each got one, the full performance, 'cause there're several others, last performance for them, like me, leaving the program. I'm so happy about not having to go to district, and nationals, with our performances."

"Yeah, so much time, energy, and parent help needed, what about Isabella and Sophia?"

"Gotcha, palfriend, I know you really like them both. They're committed, will stay on with the dancing for awhile. Hey, we'll do stuff, the four of us, until you get the guts to ask one of them out on a real date."

"You know my plan."

He gave her his steady gaze and smiled to her.

"Uh huh, you're not ready yet."

ℰↄ

Audra looked over the note she wanted to send with the pin to the national sorority headquarters, information Miss Chamberlain gave her several weeks before. She checked over her penmanship and spelling.

Dear National Headquarters,

My Ephrine High counselor, Celia Chamberlain, gave me information about what to do with this sorority pin, which I am returning to you. I found the pin among my dad's possessions as I helped remove a few of his things a year after he died, this past Christmas holiday. My hope is that you might find Madalyn and return the pin to her (if that is possible). I would appreciate it if you NOT share any information about me; I need to remain anonymous. Please let my counselor know you got the pin via her e-mail. (Then she'll let me know).

My counselor (who was in a sorority in college) says a sorority pin is a very precious possession. I have no knowledge of who this Madalyn is. And I am letting you know that my mother, Ashley, has no knowledge of this whole situation. I am sending this package completely on my own. I have a fear, a kinda weird feeling, about this pin. I'm really relieved to return it to you and thanks for helping me.

*   Sincerely,*

*   Audra Davisson*

She rode her bike to the Package Store and asked for a padded envelope.

"I'm enclosing the pin wrapped in plastic, my note and a copy of the e-mail Miss Chamberlain gave me. Once I address the envelope and add my return address, then all I gotta do is pay up," she blew out a breath before she approached the cashier.

As she walked out of the store, she felt an acid burn from her tummy spew up into her throat.

"Shouldn't I feel better? she whispered as she unlocked her bike and headed home. "Or have I started something else, oh God, be with me; I'm just tryin' to do what I think is the right thing. I'm just real glad I took six pictures of the pins, both dad's and this lady's, together and separate, with my trusty little camera. I got those shots developed. And I put dad's pin with my three other precious things, with my gold box stuff. Now I got evidence of what I sent to national, maybe dumb, but I got the pics."

She remembered an adage from her Granddad Tsosie, "No good deed goes unpunished."

She got off her bike and pushed it along on the sidewalk, almost the whole way home, those words unnerving her.

℘

"Mom, news, I've got great news."

Ashley laid her coat and briefcase on the kitchen island.

"Tell me, dear Dra."

Audra hugged her mom, "I'm Elaine, in *Arsenic and Old Lace*."

"Oh Audra, that's wonderful, it's the part you wanted, right?"

"It is; our play director did such a great job of casting the play, especially the Brewster sisters, Abby and Martha. Two of our funniest girls in the junior class are gonna play those roles. They'll do just awesome as the old aunties."

"I'm trying to remember, Elaine loves a young man, and I think they get married."

"That's right, Elaine's the girl next door."

"And the young man, uh, wasn't his name Mortimer?"

Ashley smiled to her daughter as Audra nodded her head.

"Right again, Mom, gosh, what a memory, there's all kinda craziness in this play. I know it'll be fun for all."

"What's the timeline, practices, stuff?"

"Four weeks, then a week off at Spring Break, then we perform Friday and Saturday nights the week after that, early April."

༄

Audra sat down at the Great Oaks piano and began playing and humming "You Are My Sunshine."

"This's the second Saturday, wonder if word got out?" she asked herself. "We had a good turnout last Saturday. Folks had a good time."

She turned and waved to her singers standing with music in their hands. She clapped and smiled as they completed the song.

"Wanta try one without the piano?"

She saw some heads nod. She stood away from the piano and toward the singers. After she gave them the chord, they began the song. She noticed him, a young person standing next to one of the elderly singers. Audra recognized the lady from last week. She took another look at the young man. They finished the song and Audra began the second verse.

"It's Mortimer, I mean Ben, oh my gosh," she thought after they completed the song.

The group sang one more song with her piano accompaniment. Claps and cheers went out among the singers when the song completed.

"This is gonna be a lot of fun, big time," they said among themselves and then to Audra.

As she collected the music from the singers, she watched Ben and the lady move toward her.

"Hi Ben."

"Hi Audra."

"Meet my grandma, Frances Ann."

Audra extended her hand and shook his grandma's hand.

"Hi Frances Ann, what do you think?"

Audra noticed the lady's twinkling blue eyes, "I love the singing; you really know how to get us charged up to sing."

Audra smiled to her and nodded.

"Grandma, Audra is the girl I told you about, from the play."

"You're Elaine, oh how I love that play. Are you still setting it in the 1940's as when it was written?"

"Yes, we're staying true to the time period, the appropriate costumes for the time, the two aunties, they'll have their white hair wigs fixed in the fashion of that era. I'm especially happy 'cause I get to wear nice dresses."

Frances stepped to Audra, "I look forward, like the dickens, to see the play. I'm coming Saturday night, with Ben's folks; Ben's dad is my boy."

"Well, we got a long way to go to get ready."

Frances smiled to her and touched Audra's shoulder, "You'll be ready, I know Ben," she turned to her grandson. "He'll help make it happen."

After the first week of play practices Audra made a decision.

"I'll do more of this. I love it on the stage, just as I did when I danced. But it's nice to use my voice."

At the end of the last practice of the second week Ben and Audra went to their play director. They practiced and were ready to ask her.

"Mrs. Maller, may we show you something from Act I? We've got a song we've written, would like to see what you think."

Ben and Audra took her back behind the set, where a piano sat. Ben explained where they thought the song might go. Mortimer and Elaine spoke their lines and before their embrace, they came together and held hands, singing the several sentences before the chorus of their song.

The chorus:

A   G
I   love you
A   G
I   love you
F   E   D
Marry   me?
C   E   G   C   E G
I will,   Oh   I will.

They smiled to each other and high fived after they walked away from their presentation. Later in the practice Mrs. Maller called them back.

"Ben and Audra, can you stay for a minute?"

They nodded as they stood near their director. The other cast members headed for home.

"Please, is our scene in?" Ben asked Mrs. Maller in a quiet voice.

"Just watching you, the loveliness of that scene you two created, and the music, your superb voices," she nodded and smiled to them, "I'm definitely adding that to the production."

Ben and Audra hugged and went to Mrs. Maller and hugged her.

≈

"After church today, want to talk to you, something your dad and I discussed awhile ago, for you, and something about me. I said I'd talk about it earlier; time's gotten away from me."

Audra held her mom's hand as they left church. They stopped to visit with their minister.

"How're you two getting along?"

Audra spoke up, "Time's helping, thanks, and we're very busy."

"That's right, Audra's got a ton going on, a school play, singing with folks at Great Oaks, and of course her school work."

"Great news," he smiled as he shared, "take good care of yourselves, we love your singing, you with our young people, Audra."

"We're all with God," Ashley nodded to their reverend as they walked away.

After they ate a late lunch, Audra started in on her homework at the little desk in her room.

"Can we have that chat?" her mom asked as she knocked on Audra's partly closed door.

"Sure, I'll make up some coffee, sit at the kitchen island?"

"Good."

"Homework's going along, about another half hour, Mom?"

"Sounds good."

After Audra made the coffee, Ashley poured a cup for both of them as they settled in their chairs, with cookies nearby.

"Haven't told you lately, 'cause you got so much, the play, Great Oaks, the kids choir, singing, your school work. I'm so proud of all you do, Audra, in addition to the cooking, cleaning, and laundry. Well, since Toby resigned, you're doing it all."

"I'm really happy, Mom, I have purpose, challenges, learning time management which is what I want, to help you out, also our community."

"So, Dra, I know you want to work, to make money, but I just want you to keep on doing what you're doing. I'm going to give you an allowance, for all you do around our home. You've got a checking account, which you haven't used. This'll be a little money management exercise, like you learned in Girl Scouts. You may want to deposit some of your allowance in your checking account. You need a checking account, for college coming up, uh, and eventually a credit card. So now is a good time to start."

"Wow, Mom," Audra's eyes widened as she gazed at Ashley, "I'm really pleased to hear that."

Ashley saw her daughter's wide smile, "There's more, dear girl."

"Oh?"

"Dad left us, well, comfortable, with his investments, but especially the insurance money. He had insurance on himself, for if something ever happened," she stopped and shook her head, "which it has."

Audra heard the shakiness in her mom's voice and watched the tears gush from her mom's dark eyes.

"She's still grieving," is all Audra could think of.

Audra put her arm across her mom's shoulders and remained quiet.

After a little while Ashley turned to her daughter, "It still comes in waves, the grief, but not like it used to."

Audra nodded to her mom.

"Our home's completely paid off, mortgage free. All I have to be concerned about now is upkeep, paying taxes and insurance. Your college education money's been set aside, to be used only for your schooling. And there's another little fund, for later on, after you've worked for a bit. Pick your school, pick your future career, it's what your dad and I want for you. There's dad's car you'll drive next year, so I've set aside for that. I continue to keep current plates, insurance and registration on it. I'll ask for your help with a little of the insurance when you start driving. It's very expensive, car insurance for a teen."

"For sure, I'm just glad it's a little bit older car, insurance and everything, not quite so expensive."

"And Audra, you know I filled in for your dad, on the city council, until they could have an election. I'm being encouraged to run for public office. I don't want city or county government. I work close with a lot of those folks."

"Oh Mom, state government?"

"Uh huh, but not until you're further along in school. I must get my attorney's office the way I want it operating. The paralegal I brought on board is doing a fine job. Before long I'll bring on a lawyer. My problem is."

As her mom searched for her words, Audra got up and poured them more coffee.

"Share, only if you want to."

"I'm thinking of a commitment that would keep me away from you from January through March."

"That's not long, what'cha thinking about?"

"This is sorta farfetched, but I want to serve my country. I can't do it in the military, but I can do it, now for my state, and who knows, someday, to represent my state, involving whole country issues."

"Oh, Mom, that sounds totally awesome. I don't think it's farfetched at all. Are, gosh, are you thinking of running for State Assembly?" Audra asked as she smiled to her mom.

"I've given it some thought."

"House or Senate?"

"Not sure, House is huge, 180, we're in District 143. The representative's been at it for a long time."

"Think it might be that the person's getting ready to retire?

"Dunno, but I've been approached to consider filing to run for the seat."

"Oh Mom, that sounds super exciting. You've been practicing law for awhile, know the issues. And you learned a lot about city involvements, while you served in dad's place."

"Once again, and I'm projecting ahead, the state legislature meets for three months, January through March and occasionally runs into April. Sessions are Monday through Friday, with stuff hanging over nights, sometimes on weekends."

"Mom, if it happens, I know what we can do, have maybe a graduate student from Humphrey University live with us for spring semester, until I'm away at school."

Ashley smiled to her daughter, "My dear, you're thinking way ahead, I had just started considering that." She paused, "Oh my goodness, I have to apply, get known, do political stuff, and get elected."

Audra giggled to her mom, "You gotta consider every possibility, oh Mom."

"More studying?"

"Yeah, I gotta get back to it, but Mom, you sure have made me feel better. I kinda know where I'm headed, uh, the whole money situation, and it sure sounds like it's a bright future for you."

❧

Audra felt her whole body shake as the dress rehearsal of the play began.

"I'm so glad most of my stuff's near the beginning."

Her fearfulness gave way to calm. It was Ben. She listened to his flawless speaking and body presentation. He carried the play so well, their singing together in the love scene. Audra loved that scene. It segued into Mortimer and Elaine marrying at Halloween. The dark comedy carried on through the acts filled with mayhem and craziness.

Her acting part kept Audra in an emotional high of well being through all the play presentations, even to the start of striking the set on that Saturday night.

"I'm pretty sure of one thing," she told herself as she helped dismantle a set. "I'm in love with Ben. That singing, saying that I love him, then the wedding scene, I can't believe it. And I wonder if he feels anything for me. I see something in his eyes, but I don't know."

A group of parents with actors and helpers in the play brought pop and pizza for the hungry crew as they began. Everyone ate plus the stage got cleared. The group agreed on their favorite scene, and the appropriate actors recreated it.

"It's late; tomorrow's church and other commitments; your parents must get you home," Mrs. Maller insisted as the cast and helpers began to meet up with their folks who came to pick them up.

Ashley helped with the pizza effort and watched her daughter all the while. Audra kept a big smile on her face.

"She's loving every second of this time," Ashley mused as they got ready to leave.

Audra held her bags with one hand and held her mother's with the other as they walked out into the cloudy April night.

"Ah, Mom, the spring smells, the lilacs, they tickle our noses."

They stood together by the car, "Mom, how can I ever thank you for all the nights you picked me up with my bike?"

"You can't, you're my joy, Audra, it was my supreme pleasure. Remember, I got to peek in to see how everyone was progressing in the play. You guys all came a really long way, from the first few practices."

"Yeah, that's for sure."

❧

Audra looked at the kitchen clock. She finished her breakfast standing up as she glanced at the front page of the Ephrine paper.

"I gotta hustle; the little children will be waiting for me at the library."

She read the cut line under the picture on the right column. **Assistant Ephrine Mayor, Christine Romerville and son, Chip, welcomed Assistant Macon Mayor, Madalyn Somner and daughter, Abby, to the celebration of the two cities' birthdays**. Audra glanced at the article that finished two pages later. She looked again at the picture of the four smiling people.

"Oh my gosh," she spoke out, "the girl, she could be me, the dark hair and eyes. The mom, oh she's dark headed too."

Audra reread the bold printed names under the picture. She couldn't catch her breath. She tried but she felt like she was about to faint. She saw dark black outlines around everything she looked at. Audra plopped down hard in a chair at the kitchen island.

"Madalyn Somner," she put her head down on her hands, "Madalyn Somner."

"Help me, God, that's the name, that's the name on the pin I found attached to my dad's pin."

Audra tried to concentrate as she read the story to the 4 and 5 year olds that hot and sunny Tuesday in July. At the end of the book, she sang a made-up song about the story. She got the idea after she read the book several times, in preparation for reading it to the children.

"I just have a tune rolling around in my head, so I write down the words and notes. It all comes together with a little singing and dance," she told the children's librarian after the little ones left the reading area.

"Honey, you've really got a gift; do you keep the lyrics and musical notes for all the efforts you do?"

"That's right, I have a little collection, especially since I work with an a cappella kid's choir at my church."

"Keep up your efforts, your song writing efforts, please."

The librarian smiled to Audra.

"I will, I will keep writing and singing."

∽

She found her way to the phone book area of the Ephrine Library after she rode her bike there. She just returned her library books and told herself she would get more. Her mom went in to the office that Saturday morning to do some catch up work.

"I wonder if this Madalyn has a land line?" Audra questioned.

She found a recent Macon phone book in the stacks of phone books.

"Oh my gosh, it's here, how lucky."

Audra took down the phone number, street address and Macon zip code. The name in the book was M. Somner, like the last name in the newspaper article.

"God, this may be meant to be. It's such a different name, the spelling, I think, well, it might be the same person the pin belongs to. But the pin, I sure did the right thing," she told herself.

Audra spent a half hour finding books she wanted to read, including several from a suggested reading list for her junior English class. She strapped on her heavy backpack and headed home on her bike. She sat at her little desk after she set out her books and ran her finger over the information she wrote down at the library.

"I'm gonna write Abby Somner. Gosh, I hope that's her last name. Maybe she'll understand, maybe she'll be, gosh I don't know what. Maybe if we could call each other, another step for me, answering why dad had Abby's mom's pin?"

Audra put her head down on her desk.

"Dad, oh dad, I watched you ride upon the clouds on my way home from the library. Please stay with me as I do this search. It's all about you, your actions; I wish I could talk to you."

She felt tears gushing from her eyes. She raised her head and wiped her eyes and nose.

"I gotta head out and mow. 'Cause this afternoon I got Senior Sing. This summer we're meeting just every other week, then back at it this fall."

All that afternoon, after Senior Sing, the letter she wanted to write whirled about in her head. That evening, after going out to dinner with her mom and her mom's best girlfriend, she wrote it.

Dear Abby,

My name is Audra Davisson, and I live in Ephrine, Georgia (it's a little bit smaller city than Macon, more southwest). A few days ago I read a column in our newspaper, about a birthday celebration of our two cities, Ephrine and Macon. There was a picture with the article, it was of you and your mom (assistant mayor of Macon) and of a boy and his mom (assistant mayor of Ephrine). I got your address and phone number from the Macon phone book at our Ephrine Library.

The article named you and your mom, and the folks from Ephrine. Here's what's happened. My dad, William Davisson, died in November, nearly two years ago. During the Christmas holiday last year my mom, Ashley, asked me to clear out a couple of drawers in my parents' closet, drawers with stuff of my dad's that needed to be sent to a nonprofit. Hidden in the top of a small container of dad's stuff I found two pieces of jewelry hooked together. They were my dad's fraternity pin (he went to Auburn) attached to a sorority pin and the Greek letters of the sorority chapter. I didn't know what to do with these two items 'cause I had a strange feeling about them. I did not share with my mom about this. Instead I asked for the confidential help of my school counselor, a woman I really trust. She helped me. And she told me how precious a sorority pin often is to a woman. She contacted the national headquarters of this sorority. I did what they wanted after I snapped pictures of the pins I found. I returned the pin to national. Your mom's name, MADALYN SOMNER, was engraved in tiny letters on the back side of the sorority pin plus a date, 11-01-81.

I don't know how your mom's sorority pin ended up hidden in my dad's stuff. If you can call me, here's my number, 304-555-3579. I am 15, will be 16 on Christmas. I was shocked when I saw the picture of you in our newspaper. You and me, well we really look alike. So by the newspaper article I know your mom is an assistant mayor. My mom is a lawyer here in Ephrine. So our moms are public figures. Again, I've shared none of this info with my mom. I think we need to talk, if it's possible. The phone number in the book for you is 770-555-1417. I just don't know what all this means. Oh, I almost always pick up our mail and leave it out for mom to look at. A letter from you, I'll keep it private, just for me. Thanks.

  Sincerely,

  Audra Davisson

The week before Audra left for Helena she got a letter.

Dear Audra,

  I'm so sorry about your dad. Yes, we need to talk and keep writing. That is the land line number for my mom and me. Here's when it's best to talk (for a short time 'cause long distance is real expensive) Wednesday and Friday mornings, my mom is almost always at her assistant mayor's office during those times, rest of time she's at her law office. I wouldn't even attempt to contact you by e-mail. I'm not saying anything to my mom right now either.

  In the mail a few months ago my mom's sorority pin came to her from her national. She seemed super happy about having it returned to her. Hey, now I know some of the back story on that!

  Not going to believe this, but my birthday is Christmas, born same year as you. I'll be a junior at Annunciation High in Macon, private Catholic high school. My mom, Madalyn, is a single parent, never married. What she tells me is that my dad was a donor (sperm, that she picked). I've accepted that. I have a wonderful mom who is for sure both mom and dad to me, gives me the love, care, and support I need. I consider myself super lucky and BLESSED to have her in my life. It won't be long before I'll be able to drive, get myself to school. Right now I get along with my bike, not that far away from school. And thank goodness I no longer need a babysitter/nanny.

  Oh, history on my mom, she's an Auburn alum; you know about the sorority, a U. of Virginia Law graduate, class of 1987. Your letter says your mom's a lawyer. When did she graduate law, what school, and what about your dad, yeah I know he at least was in a fraternity at Auburn and it sounds like he and my mom, connected by pins, serious? Like you I always pick up our mail. I really want to meet you. For me too, I don't know what this all means.

Sincerely,

Abby Somner (Abigail, I'm named after my mom's sister who died early)

Dear Abby,

Thanks for your quick response. I'm flying out to Helena, MT to spend a week with my grandparents in two days. But I wanted to try to answer questions. My folks both graduated from the U. of Virginia Law in 1988. Mom graduated U. of Alaska before law school. They married and you know about me, Christmas Day, 1990, just like your birth date. My granddad Davisson wanted my dad, Will, to join him in his Montgomery, Alabama law firm, after dad graduated. He chose mom, a smaller community in Georgia (Ephrine), and a law firm which mom and dad established as soon as they moved here. The firm got busy really fast. So they had me, the firm, hands full. And about the pin, my high school counselor (also in a sorority in college), when I showed her the connected pins, well she said that there's an actual ceremony, called a pinning, when a girl and guy get, like, pre-engaged. I guess it's really beautiful. I wonder if your mom and my dad, if that's what happened to them. Will we ever know? Maybe one day your mom may share. I don't know if you've got anyone to talk to about this. I'm gonna share with my grandparents in Helena. If anybody understands, they will and they'll not say a word. They're great folks, Inuit (Eskimo), came from Nome, Alaska to Helena when mom was a little girl. Let's not write again until I can call you after I get back from Montana. (Like if mom sees a letter from you, yeah, I'm not ready to face that)!

Sincerely,

Audra

಄

"So dear Audra, what's been your favorite place so far on this trip here?"

"Grandma, I think the hike we took overlooking your beautiful Helena Valley, that'd be first, then kinda a tie between visiting the original Governor's Mansion, and the Cathedral of St. Helena."

"We thought you might be old enough to enjoy the beauty of the architecture in both the mansion and the cathedral."

"What I can't believe is how wonderful it is to have those two landmarks, two so positively gorgeous places, up here in the wild and wooly high West area."

Her grandma laughed, "That's right, Audra, we have special and different locations, some natural and some built by man's own hands. And for your last day here?"

"Horseback riding with you and granddad tomorrow morning, go to our favorite place for lunch, and play games in the afternoon, early to bed. Then I gotta pack and you must get me to the airport early."

"Anything else?"

"Uh huh, Grandma, I gotta share what's on my mind. You need to tell granddad."

They held hands as they went for a walk around her grandparents' neighborhood.

Audra looked up at the cloudy sky, said a prayer and plunged in. After she explained the pin situation and the letters she and Abby wrote, she shared her fear with her grandma.

"The picture in the paper, Grandma, I thought I was looking at myself. Uh, maybe dad cared for two different women, one he knew from school (like Madalyn and the pinning), and mom at Virginia Law. I have a suspicion that Abby and I, well, may be related. But all this is just my teenage speculation. What it'll do is really make mom sad, if this doesn't come out well."

"That's right, it will. We need to be very careful about this whole situation, Audra. Your granddad and I'll try to help, especially with your mom. And if you can think of Abby's mom, raising Abby, being both parents, wanting just her daughter in her life."

"Yeah, I've heard of women raising kids on their own, just not folks around me, well until now, uh, mom's a single parent. So I know firsthand there are single women everywhere raising children alone. And mom shared something with me which was a surprise. You remember she finished up a term of dad's, when he was on the Ephrine City Council?"

"I do, your mom really stepped up, because she also had the law firm to deal with, plus you. You two really grieved. Your granddad and I, we pray every day for you and your mom. Early on, after you lost your dad, we prayed about getting your feet on the ground, moving ahead. Now the challenges are much bigger, you going away to school in some months, her firm growing. Sorry, sweetie, I got away from the City Council."

"Mom, she's been asked, and she's really thinking about, running for the State Assembly."

Audra turned to her grandma, nodding her head.

"Really?"

Her grandma stopped walking. Audra watched her questioning eyes shine like black pools.

"Oh my goodness, Audra, wouldn't that be something." She paused, "She's not said a word about that. And I'll wait for her to tell me before I mention anything."

"Please share this and my other information about Abby with granddad."

"Audra, pray for your dad, too. I don't know what was going on in his life way back before you were born. I've made huge mistakes in my life. It is not our place to judge; not judge others, just take care of ourselves."

They continued their walk, rounding the corner back toward the Tsosie home. Audra put her arm around her grandma's shoulders.

"Thank you for listening to me; I just have so much on my mind."

Before they walked into her home grandma and Audra hugged.

"Audra, try to let all this go from your mind, enjoy the rest of your summer, helping out with lunches at the shelter, reading to the children at the library, your Senior Sing, oh and there's Ben." She paused, "God's with you, darling girl, with me and all of us, do you understand, it's His Will for us?"

"Grandma, I'll try."

⅋

After Ashley picked Audra up at the Atlanta airport, they drove north to the Midtown area of Atlanta.

"Treating you to dinner out and a stay at a hotel for tonight. We haven't done this since before your dad died, Audra."

At dinner Audra shared several of her favorite times while she was with her grandparents.

"I was so happy that granddad took a day off, to be with us, to ride horses, just gentle-like, that's the way they are with me, gentle, laid back. And grandma and I, hiking, oh Mom, she's in super great shape; you've got her beautiful figure, posture, so striking."

"Just like you, my beautiful daughter, I see me, and your grandma, in you. But your dad's all over in your face, the shape, his nose, his round eyes that are yours, yours are so dark and his, such a bright blue. Mine, my eyes, so black, quite slanted."

Audra held her hand as Ashley put her hand out to her across the tablecloth.

"To me, Mom, it's an oriental feature of your face. Like Jeff says, 'you're exotic.'"

Ashley began to giggle at Audra's remark.

"Oh Mom, he's really got an eye, for a pretty woman. You know, when we get home, he'll be driving."

"That's gonna be tough for you, but thank goodness you'll be in driving school. And at Christmas, oh, a day or so after, you'll be able to go without me being along."

"I can wait; I'll just get lazy, go everywhere in the car, when I should be riding my bike."

Audra watched her mom just nod her head and smile to her.

℘

"I sure hope it's just Abby at home."

Audra remembered the best times to call Abby. Once again she got lucky. After the teens talked, it became clear, especially to Audra that they should keep writing. After a couple of letters over several months, Abby told Audra by phone that she wanted to meet Audra, and to talk to her mom, Madalyn, about the whole situation.

As it happened, Audra's mom needed to be in Atlanta for both a lawyer's conference, and to talk with the District 143 representative. On that Saturday afternoon in October Abby and Madalyn met Audra at her home in Ephrine.

"I'm scared to death," Audra spoke out as she looked at herself in the bathroom mirror.

She just brushed her hair and applied a little mascara on her thick black eyelashes. She headed down the stairs and made the pot of coffee, digging out the cookies she made earlier in the day. She also had several cans of pop, in case Abby liked pop. She already planned to be absent from Senior Sing and had one of the singers handle the sing that day.

Audra heard the doorbell ring, at the appointed time they said they'd be at her home. Emotion smacked Audra hard in her head. She teared up as she whispered, "What have I done?"

She opened the door and stood in the foyer as they entered.

"Welcome," she smiled to Madalyn and Abby Somner.

Abby and Audra hugged and stood back from each other.

They both shook their heads, and Audra whispered, "Unbelievable."

Audra then stepped to Madalyn and held out her hand.

"I'm Audra, Madalyn."

They shook hands.

"She's distraught," is all Audra could think of as she looked over the woman's face.

"I, I really need to sit down," Madalyn croaked out as she started to cry.

Audra took their jackets as Abby led her mom to the big kitchen island. She helped her mom sit down. The teens watched tears gush from Madalyn's eyes.

Audra put the plate of cookies on the island counter in front of their chairs.

"Coffee, ladies?"

"Oh yes, please, for both of us," Abby spoke out.

"Black?"

"Yes."

Audra poured out three cups of coffee in Christmas mugs she used all year long.

"How was your drive?"

"Good, Abby drove most of the way. Are you driving with your mom?"

"I am, I can't wait for day after Christmas, to get my license."

Abby laughed, "Oh my gosh, me too, it'll be my best Christmas present."

"Abby, thank you for your letters and calls, and for getting your mom to meet me."

"I know you're just not ready to have all this flung at your mom, Audra."

"For sure."

"Abby and I've talked a little, but I just want to share, just one time, about your dad and me, Audra."

Audra finished her coffee and poured herself another cup. They finished off their cups too, and she filled up theirs.

"I'm fortified now," Madalyn exclaimed after she ate a cookie.

"Will and I dated at Auburn, his junior year, and my senior year. He broke up with the girl he'd gone to high school and on to Auburn with. That was maybe six or so months before he met me. My reaction to him, one amazing dude, almost instant desire, wanted to meld our hearts together, I thought, forever. We got pinned, almost immediately. It was an awesome, beautiful ceremony, with my sisters and his fraternity brothers singing to us." She paused, "I took my LSAT's, got admitted to Virginia Law. He still had to get through senior year, and figure out for sure what he wanted to do with the rest of his life."

"I ended it, the night after I graduated. I loved," she turned to Audra, "your dad, beyond anything I'd ever experienced. But I had a burning desire to become a lawyer that trumped everything else in my life. I handed him my sorority pin and his fraternity pin, entwined together. I remember watching him put the pins in his suit jacket pocket. I'll never forget what he told me then."

"'Madalyn,' he said in a determined voice, his blue eyes sparkling, 'I want to be a lawyer. I'm leaving the fraternity, gonna study my ass off to get ready for the test, I'm serious. You, you helped me realize my dream, your example that I now want, my Juris Doctorate.'"

"I didn't see your dad again, for years. For some reason, all the time at Virginia Law, I never ran into him, maybe 'cause it was a three year program, and my third year, super intense, sometimes doing the real stuff, gone from campus some."

"I ended up in Atlanta, at a lawyer conference, in March 1989. I'd decided, after dating several guys in Macon, that I needed to settle down. I wanted a baby, but I didn't want a guy in my life. I tried to get pregnant with two different guys. No luck, so I got frustrated and gave myself a timeout from trying to have a baby. I decided maybe to use a sperm donor. Then at the last night of the conference there was a dinner party for all involved. I sat down at the table where my nametag indicated. As I looked up and across I saw Will, with that fabulous smile, looking as handsome and youthful as he had in college. That was it. All those old feelings, the intensity of what we felt for each other, came back for me. The next morning we ate breakfast together, shared what had happened to us over the years. He headed back to Ephrine, and I returned to Macon."

"When I found out I was pregnant, at first I wanted to abort." She turned to her daughter and touched her shoulder. "But as you grew inside me, Abby, I knew this was what I'd wanted all my life, a career, but also a baby. All along, I never wanted a husband. I decided at your birth that I was your mother, but also your father. I would raise you alone, as I'd always desired. And that's the way it's been. And that's the way it always will be."

Abby and Audra looked at each other, so close in size, in height, hair color.

"Abby's eyes are hazel, lighter than mine," Audra saw, "and my skin color, slightly darker."

In the face, Madalyn saw Will, in both Abby and Audra. She turned first to her daughter, and then turned the other way to Audra.

"There is no mistaking it," she told herself.

"I, I been seeing a guy, my age, and I really like him a lot. And so, Madalyn, I say to you, that the emotion of wanting to be one, with a guy, that's just about the strongest, the most powerful emotion I've ever felt. And I'm just a kid. So I can begin to understand, how what you and my dad, well, I can understand. Dad had to live with what he'd done. And it's none of my business, I cannot judge, cannot judge, anyone, but myself. But he never knew, about Abby?"

"There was never a communication between your dad and me after that conference," Madalyn nodded to Audra.

"So I do have a dad, and he's died," Abby paused. "So Mom, as you've told me so many times, you are my dad, and you are my mom. You love me, and I love you."

"What now?"

The three women sat together in silence.

"First, Abby, I'm so glad you've shared what you and Audra've done, the writing letters, the phone calls. And Abby, it took huge courage for you to tell me that Audra's dad died."

Madalyn paused and took a deep breath, "That had to be a terrible hard thing, Audra, for you and your mom. I know your mom's still grieving. Will, he was an amazing, well, you know Audra. What I'm concerned about is somehow gently letting your mom know about all of this. I could use some advice."

"For both of you, I've talked to my wonderful grandparents, mom's folks, up in Montana. They know about some of this, and they stay in touch with me. What you need to know is that mom is thinkin' really seriously of running for the State Assembly, in the House. It's one of the reasons she's out of town right now, to talk with the older man who's in her district, the representative. I don't know if somethin' like this is going to set my mom back."

"You know what I think?"

"What, Abby?" Madalyn asked.

"I think it's time for Audra and me to get to know each other better. And I think, Mom, that you and Ashley need to get together and talk. You should meet her face to face."

Audra watched the serious concern on Abby's face as she spoke to her mom.

"I wonder if that will really happen," Audra thought to herself.

She felt a rip of acid burn her tummy.

"Thank you for that, Abby, I'm making a promise to you girls; I will have that talk with Ashley. Please, Audra, let me tell your mother. It's my place, not yours. You've done the proper thing, returning my sorority pin to national. And then me, the pin returned, to me. That was an unbelievable gift, and I thank you for that, Audra."

Madalyn touched Audra's shoulder, "You, you've helped me get my life straightened out. I only wish I hadn't been so selfish, not telling Will."

Abby added, "About me."

"Dad and I talk a lot. Believe me, he knows, hey he's here with us, right now, right here," Audra smiled to Madalyn and Abby.

℘

"I'll just want to sing in this production."

"You could be the lead, Audra," Ben smiled to her as they sat together in a booth at the cozy café Audra liked.

"I'm in the background on this one. I've got my eye on *Brigadoon.*

"That's community theater, in the spring?"

"Uh huh, I want to try for Fiona, who falls for Tommy. There's dance, and singing, and speaking parts, the whole deal, Ben."

"It'll be your turn to shine, Audra."

She turned to him, "Your turn's right now, with *High School Musical.*

"It is, 'cause I want to do track in the spring."

"What event?"

"Hurdles."

"You're way tall."

"That's why I do them, I just let my legs fly up."

"Do you even feel your feet touch the ground?"

"Nah, such a high."

"Kinda like what I feel when I hike."

"That's it."

"I gotta get you home; I got homework, like big time."

"So do I; I just, well, super like spending time with you. We're so gosh darn busy. And I especially like that we're both in this fall musical. Ben, you got so much talent, I hope you get to do something with all that ability once you decide where you're headed, I mean to school."

Audra felt Ben touch her hand and rub it, "It's what I, well, I appreciate so much about you, Audra, you're so encouraging, so positive, in the way you talk to me. You really care."

She touched his cheek with her free hand, "I really do."

She felt his sky blue eyes search her brown eyes.

"Pools of shining dark waters, I could swim in your eyes, Audra."

Audra watched him let out a deep breath as he let go of her hand.

They walked hand in hand out of the café.

"So much ahead of us."

"Right, Ben, thanks for our time together," she squeezed his hand, turned and smiled to him.

"It's my supreme pleasure."

3

Christmas 2006-Junior year

"I got my license, Dad, I'm coming out to you, something I been wanting to do for over a year."

Two days after Christmas Audra waited until after her mom headed to the law firm. She remembered the directions to a community cemetery, Pine View. As she got out of the car, she looked up to see the sun peek through the clouds, warming her as she moved to her dad's gravestone. She held the Christmas wreath in her hands. She remembered the conversation. The florist asked her what she wanted on the wreath.

"Only pinecones, maybe a tiny bird figure or two. My dad, he loved the outdoors."

"Got it, I wrote down your instructions."

Audra heard herself say that she would be happy with what the florist fixed up. And she was.

"Oh Dad, I'm placing the wreath against your gravestone. It is a beautiful wreath, and I'm so happy I can finally bring it to you where your ashes rest. I just couldn't last year, not old enough to drive or do much of any of the things I can do now, hey, now that I'm 16. And your dad and mom visited, but, yeah, you know that. It was wonderful because both mom and me, well we needed cheering up. And your folks, well, they did that for us, they cheered us. I love you. And tonight, it's my birthday celebration. I know you'll be with me there, looking down at the happy gathering."

Audra started to walk away. She stopped, remembered another thought, and returned to the grave.

She spoke out, "Dad, Madalyn is meeting with mom in a few days. I'm praying hard for mom. It'll throw her off for awhile. I know you didn't know about Abby. But now you do. Stay with us, dad, Abby, me, well we need you. You're our dad. I wish, oh I wish, that you have eternal peace."

Audra walked around the back side of the grave stone. She bent over and hugged the top of it. She cried, tears dribbling down her face. Finally she rose up and mopped up her nose and eyes with a tissue.

"I'm so happy I could do this for you, Dad," she looked up into the sky again, "my Christmas present for you."

&

"Where's the birthday girl who loves desserts?

Audra raised her hand.

"As you requested," the waiter smiled to her, "red velvet cupcakes."

He passed out a cupcake to Jeff, Isabella, Ben, Sophia, and her mom after he gave her a cupcake with a single lit candle.

"There're more in the kitchen, for you to take home."

The group starting laughing as they saw the huge smile spread across Audra's face.

"More desserts, Audra, you're in heaven."

She gave eye contact to each of them and said with much emphasis, "They'll be gone by 10 a.m. tomorrow morning."

She heard laughter erupt from the entire table.

As they settled down, she heard Ben's voice, with everyone joining in, wishing her Happy Birthday. She looked up as she made her wish. Then she blew out the candle.

"Dig in."

"We did what you requested, Audra," Isabella said. "We're honoring you; we all chipped in, a gift to Shriner's Childrens Hospitals. And thanks for getting us the address for the hospital."

"I think we'd all like that to be a birthday gift, we're past presents, time to give back, help others," Jeff spoke out.

℘

"Sweet Dra, I'm headed out to meet Madalyn at the rectory."

Audra came to her mom as they stood in the kitchen together. They hugged.

"You must be OK, then, with Father from St. Luke's standing in as a mediator," she gazed into her mom's eyes.

Ashley nodded, "Yes, totally OK, Madalyn's Catholic; I'll defer to her on this situation. I'm really glad you've not shared with me, Audra. I need to hear what this woman has to say. I need to listen, that's my strong suit. Being a lawyer I hear my client."

"So I'm sayin' what you told me to say to you, Mom; keep your mouth shut until Madalyn's shared. And Mom, please call your folks when you get back home. They been guiding me through some of this stuff. They know what you're gonna know."

Ashley nodded, "OK, I will, I'll call them."

℘

After her mom left, Audra went to her room, got down on her knees and prayed and talked to God for a long time. She wiped away the tears that burned her eyes.

"I need to eat; Mom told me to fix myself soup and toasted cheese."

Audra felt better after she fixed herself that favorite meal. Her mom had not said when she would be home.

"I'll watch my favorite romance story, 'cause school's coming and it's gonna be a crazy semester, no time to watch then."

Half way through the movie her mom came home. Audra had coffee ready, and a plate of cookies, their comfort food. A few minutes later Ashley sat down at the kitchen counter with her daughter.

Audra turned and directed her eyes to her mom's. She put her arm around her mom's shoulders and held her for a brief time.

"Talk to me, Mom."

They both swallowed big draughts of coffee.

Audra heard her mom blow at a big breath, "Thank you Audra for everything you've done, that led to this meeting with Madalyn, and learning about Abby. You really are quite a detective."

"Uh huh, but I had help, people who guided me about what to do."

"Yes, now I know. I'll proceed on with my plans for you, for me, for us. I'm not going to be blindsided by information I did not know."

"That's right, Mom, the reason I did all this, to let you be informed. I want you to be that public official I think you need to be, part of the state assembly."

"And Audra, I've forgiven Madalyn, for what happened. As I told her and Father, I can't judge, I won't judge, I don't know what I would have done, had I been in Madalyn's shoes. My sadness," she started to cry and Audra grabbed tissues for her, "is for dear Abby."

"Mom, you haven't met her yet, but you will. Abby and I've become friends. And she's doing really well, never had a dad, and her mom seems like a super strong lady, like you. Abby really loves her mom, that's what they've shown me when I was with them. Don't be sad for Abby, she's strong, like her mom, like me. God's caring for all of us, Mom. We have our faith, our hope, and our love for Him, for our family, for dad. I consider Abby a member of my family now."

They each stood up from their chairs, moved away from them and hugged.

"I have to give this whole situation time, to let it sink into my brain. I still grieve for Will. I always ask God to help me through the sadness and anger that he still invokes in me. Oh, and I have something to show you, actually give to you."

She went to her purse and pulled out a picture and placed it on the counter.

"Madalyn gave this to me. Abby wanted me to see a picture of her, and she wanted me to give it to you. I tell you Audra, when I first saw the picture, I positively gasped."

"Yeah, the same thing happened to Madalyn when she first saw me."

"You two are not twins, but you are so both your dad, completely in the face, that it's, well, it's genetics."

Audra giggled, which led to a smile she saw on her mom's face.

"And because you and Madalyn both have dark eyes and dark hair, and both tall, same body type, that just added to the alikeness of our looks, Abby and me."

"Before I head upstairs, I wanted to ask. Do you think Abby might want a picture of Will? Audra, you keep one in a locket and a picture by your bed."

"Yeah, Mom, I asked Abby about that. She said she wanted to think about it. And that's all I know."

"We'll give her some time to absorb all this."

ᐧᣟ

"I think Tommy's (that's Alex) half in love with you, Audra. Your singing, it was heartfelt, anyway I could feel the intensity of it, all through *Brigadoon*. You sure as heck got talent. I couldn't really see it in *Arsenic and Old Lace*. We just worked together so close. I know that's when I got so gobsmacked for you."

They held hands as they exited the community theater.

"One more performance, then I'm free. I'm so glad I did this show. But it'll be my last one where I'm a lead. Next year, maybe one, sometime, but definitely I'll be in the background. Hey, that's our senior year, unbelievable, how fast it's gone, Ben."

"That's 'cause we been busy. And happy, I'm so happy to spend time with you when we can. But I've also almost made a decision."

"What?"

"Not until it's clear in my brain, then I can talk it out with you, Audra."

℘

"Hey, have you got a sec?"

"You're home from practice early."

"Yeah, have you looked out; it's raining hard, too dangerous to run high hurdles, the mud."

"Gotcha."

"Hey, my grandma just called; it's why I'm calling you."

"Frances Ann?"

"Uh huh, she read me a piece from the today's local newspaper."

"OK?"

"It's about you, your talent; you blew away a reporter from the newspaper who saw one of your performances in *Brigadoon*. She had good things to say about your voice, also your dancing and singing. There's also a picture of you and Tommy dancing."

"I haven't looked at the paper today."

"You better take a look. It just confirms what I been tellin' you all along. You're super talented. And the reporter mentioned your young age and all the abilities you've gained over the years, way to go, Audra. I'll let you go 'cause I know you got practicing and homework. See you at school."

"Oh, thank you, Ben, so sweet that you called me."

As soon as they hung up, Audra found the paper where she always put it for her and her mom. She went through two sections of the paper before she found the article.

"Gosh, that was nice," Audra whispered after she read the piece. "Dad, I read it to you also." She felt tears rush to her eyes. "Dear, dear dad, I wish you could've seen one of my performances." She cried harder as she realized, "Hey, you were there with me, giving me that confidence I've gained, the initiative for each new project I tackle."

℥

"Miss Chamberlain, thanks for our talk a couple of weeks ago. I haven't told mom yet, wanted to share with you and my grandparents first."

"Auburn?"

"Right, will apply early next fall. I looked at the program I'm interested in."

"BME?"

"You've got a memory," she gazed at her counselor, nodded her head and smiled.

"I'm interested in my students, in their plans for their futures."

"And I know what that means, an audition. So besides getting admitted to Auburn, I need to submit my application to the music education program. When I do those two things, well the audition will follow."

"Do you have a timeline?"

"Uh huh, February, next year, mom'll need to drive me to Auburn, so I can participate in the auditions. I don't want to send a video. I'll get the feel for the school by showing up to do this."

"Audra, you've been performing most of your life, in dance, in voice, your piano playing, your drama work. This will be the next logical step."

"Miss Chamberlain, I want to be a secondary music educator, choral, and be able to work in drama, so I'll need those kinds of classes."

Audra watched her counselor smile to her, "I'm very proud of you, Audra, for thinking through all this."

"This summer, my whole summer will be devoted to voice and piano, I'll take lessons and practice, practice,

practice. I plan to be ready to audition by the start of school in the fall. That way, all fall, until February, I can practice what I'll need to do, all the criteria necessary for the audition. There's only one scary thing."

"What's that?" Miss Chamberlain raised her eyebrows in questioning.

"The sight reading."

Audra watched her nod and say, "So gather all your musical materials, sight read them all, no matter how simple or complicated. Sit down, play and sing, you'll have sight reading for voice, anything and everything you've not played before or sung."

"Right, I'll want to do voice and piano, so 3 ½ hours every day for each one, all summer long, every day; I'll have to do that much."

"Oh, and Audra, you might want to learn one musical instrument."

"Right, that's required for what I'm planning, actually three instruments and a percussion."

She nodded to Audra, "The more you know, the better prepared you'll be to take on a position when you apply to teach. And you know music, it'll take so much of your time, after school, practices, performances at night. I must share, you know this, schools across the country are having serious financial difficulties and there may be more hard times coming."

"Yeah, I know about all the hours, from all the night time work I've done all through the years. Thanks for reminding me of that. And yes, I'm aware that the first programs that are eliminated in the schools are the art and music situations. I'll continue to pay close attention to that. Down the road I don't want to end up at a school, build a program, and then have it eliminated. And I'll check with mom, see what she thinks for an instrument to start with for me. I'd have to decide whether I wanted to play something that'd do the melody, or an instrument that harmonized, maybe in the treble clef."

"Go to it, young lady, and by the way, thanks for keeping me updated on your family's latest scenario."

"Uh huh, it's quite a story, what a pin can do."

They hugged and Audra hurried on to her next class.

℘

"You have to do it, Ben."

"Show me what you mean."

"I love you, I really love you," she sang and danced around him. She took steps away from him, returned to him and held him close as he stood there.

"Yeah, not just words, but showing me you care by your smile and your hug."

They stood together in a park near Audra's home. She looked up to him.

"Summer theater will give you so much practice in doing that. At school we just do, like a couple productions a year. This summer, in closer order, you'd do three. It'd help you decide if drama is something you want to do, a degree in college, or just a fun other thing for you to do with spare time."

With those encouraging words Audra finished convincing Ben that he needed to get away from Ephrine to do summer theater, act, dance, sing, make sets, learn lighting, direct. Several days later she heard from him.

"It'll be so long soon, Audra. I've heard back; I'm so excited to be heading to summer theater. I'll miss you."

Audra stood at the kitchen counter near the phone, "You'll have so much going on, Ben. I'm happy for you, and I know you'll do so great."

℘

"Thanks for letting me drive, Grandma Brenda. This's been a wonderful break for me, 'cause Monday starts my lessons and seven-days-a-week practices."

"It's been our pleasure, Audra, to have you visit your grandpa and me. I was so glad you got to go to our summer place for a weekend while you were here in Alabama."

"My favorite, rowing out on the lake, with you once, and twice with grandpa. We had a chance to talk. I'm so glad you and Grandpa Clint accepted Abby. The fact that you want me to keep you updated on her, well, that's real special. She does have one set of grandparents, but it's good for her to know that she also has another set."

"Honey, pull over and I'll drive the rest of the way to Ephrine. You've done great, with your driving. And remember, Abby had no choice in her birth, just like none of us had a choice. What we have to accept is the situation we land in. Abby is fortunate to have a mom strong enough to take care of her daughter's needs. You know what, Audra?"

"What's that, Grandma?"

"I am just super proud of Abby and her mom. They are happy and they are loved, loved by each other."

Audra and her grandma switched sides with grandma driving.

"We're not that far away from your home."

"Grandma Brenda."

"What, honey?"

"Isn't that all any of us can ask for, to be happy, to love and be loved."

"That's it, Audra."

Brenda took her right hand from the steering wheel and held tight to Audra's left hand for a brief time.

Audra's grandma left early the next morning for her drive back to Montgomery. Both Audra and Ashley got up to have coffee with her and see her off. Before she left Audra showed her grandma the stacks of piano and vocal music she would practice over the summer. She also sang several lines of the Verdi piece she wanted to do for the necessary recital, the voice part.

℘

Jeff went out with the girls, Audra, Isabella, and Sophia, for movies they wanted to see at the local theater in the early part of the summer. He started to make up his mind.

Audra urged him, "Time to put your thoughts into action, whichever girl it is, for goodness sake, ask her out."

"You won't be mad at me, sad that I'm also interested in another girl in my life."

"No Jeff, I won't," she told him over the phone.

"Fourth of July."

"Yeah, Jeff, awesome, our a cappella group sang before the big barbeque and fireworks display. You were comfortable with me, then when Isabella and Sophia joined us, it didn't seem much different, right?"

"Uh huh, but it's because you were there, Audra."

"Strike out on your own, Jeff."

The phone went silent for a little bit.

"I'm gonna do it, you're givin' me the go ahead."

"Good luck, Jeff, you know I'll see Ben again, when he gets home from theater camp, right before the start of school, can you believe it, our senior year?"

"Nope, can't."

"So see ya, after I get back from Interlochen."

"You'll do great."

"Yeah, I will, you saw my audition DVD I sent them."

"I did."

℘

"I'm practicing long hours, every day. And I haven't said anything to my friends, except Jeff, about what I'm doing, my two camps."

Ashley stood with her daughter in the kitchen, fixing coffee and food for breakfast.

"That's OK, Audra, know you've been working very hard, and I know you want to do well with your piano and voice. You are, well, super lucky and blessed that your grandparents've taken such an interest in your future education, an awesome Christmas present which you're getting this summer."

Audra's Grandpa Clint and Grandma Brenda wanted to send her to special short camps during that summer. They paid for everything, tuition, room and board, and plane fare. Ashley drove her to Atlanta where Audra flew via interconnecting flights to Interlochen, near Traverse City, Michigan.

Audra used every bit of her musical knowledge to stay up with the talented students who took part in the one week piano institute. Her days exhausted her, the practices, but she loved the challenges of the musical techniques she learned. To not have to eat her own cooking and to spend a little time outside on the beautiful grounds of the institute became her favorites of this camp. Midway through the institute she called her mom and grandparents, letting them know how much she learned.

Ashley picked her up at baggage in the Atlanta airport.

"Mom, I learned one thing, super important, the world of music is huge. I'm just barely scratching the surface, of everything I know I'll learn in college."

A week later back they drove to the airport. This time Audra flew to Oberlin, OH. At this vocal academy for high school students Audra spent nine days of intensive training in voice. A couple of evenings she noticed her voice going hoarse. Audra felt very comfortable learning more about voice. She participated in several sings. She came from an a cappella background, and she found several groups that were doing that kind of performing. She caught on easily to the songs. A video final presentation of the nine day camp would go to both her mom and her grandparents. They couldn't be there for her final shows, so the DVD was the next best thing.

On their way home, Audra shared with her mom, "There're gonna be so many opportunities to watch me perform in the next few years. I'm expanding, as a teacher I may be involved in band, and orchestra, besides voice and piano."

"Now it seems like drama, acting, dance, that's just a tiny little piece in your whole world of music."

"Uh huh, I'm so grateful I've gotten to meet so many talented young people. There are a couple I intend to stay in touch with, one who thinks he may be going to Auburn."

"In your program?"

"Maybe, but he's got a lot ahead of him, being admitted to the school, and then to the program, and he's got to have an audition, just like I'm gonna do."

℘

By the end of the summer, she felt dazed, but satisfied by all the efforts she made.

"Mom, I gotta practice every day from here on out, but I think I'm ready, my vocal and piano teachers say I am. They're so glad I got to go to camp this summer. And the band director likes the way I'm taking hold of the French horn. It's got such a beautiful sound, a favorite of mine now, I think."

"I'm glad you picked an instrument and are doing so well playing it."

"And Mom," she eyed her mom as they sat having coffee and donuts together that Saturday morning, "thank you for paying for all the lessons, plus buying my instrument. I feel real fortunate I found a used horn in such good shape. I'm so grateful for everything you do for me."

"Sweet Dra, I've always wanted you to take lessons of some kind, keeps your brain and body engaged, whether it was dance, voice, drama, or piano. It's important to your total development. One of my favorite things is to see you flit about our home humming or singing a song."

"And Mom, after auditions in February, well, the sounds're gonna be screechy and scratchy."

"Oh yes, you've decided to finish your senior year learning both the violin and the clarinet."

"I gotta Mom, have to have strings, woodwind, and brass, that's my French horn, for my university classes coming up."

&

Ashley filed for District 143, on the Republican side, for the House seat. She found an empty small office space on Main Street, in the middle of Ephrine, between a flower shop and a café. It turned out to be a perfect location for her election campaign, and she rented it on the spot. Audra spent evenings at her mom's headquarters, preparing mailings, reading over speeches, helping out where she could when she wasn't studying.

A grad student from Humphrey University became Ashley's right hand man from late August on as the election began to ramp up. She took him with her to away-from-town events in her district. Grant Ellings needed to complete his internship, in time to graduate at Christmas. Ashley's venture into politics turned out to be the perfect solution for this young man's final semester in the Political Science master's program at Humphrey University. He got approval for that necessary internship to assist Ashley from his advisor and graduate committee head.

He explained to Ashley that he would take the rudimentary lessons from a suggested on-line how-to-be-elected program and shape them into what she needed, for her talks, for her message to the voters. Her all-important budget situation would need to be looked over by the appropriate State Election Budget committee. Ashley needed to account for every penny of the money coming in for her campaign. She went through a client situation like this in her law practice and knew how critical the money issue was.

And she heard from some of her constituents that her fellow Republican candidate for Seat #143 did little to help his reelection. Ashley found that strange and talked to her committee about him. And then he stepped down, deciding not to run again, at the last minute.

∾

Audra completed her voice and piano practicing for that afternoon in October. She made up a fresh pot of coffee and drank a partial cup before heading upstairs to begin her homework.

She heard the phone.

"Audra."

"Mom, whassup?"

"Oh goodness, I've gotten some news from Grant. He just heard."

"What, oh gosh, Mom?"

Audra heard the worried tone in her mom's voice. She froze in place, her tummy knotting up, and her tears starting.

"143, our rep, the man who conceded, decided not to seek reelection."

Her mom stopped talking. Audra waited, knowing her mom again tried to find her words.

"Dead."

"I'm so sorry, wow, I wonder if he was sick, and that made him decide not to run. What does this all mean, Mom?"

"I hafta get more votes than the Democrat running for our district."

"So, you gotta move forward with all the stuff you planned the next three weeks, right?"

"That's right. But, I'll need for you to go with me to the man's funeral, part of his final wishes, and yes, he was really sick."

"Got it, Mom," she paused, "seems like we just went through this ourselves."

"Right, gotta go, I'll keep you updated. It'll be a late night, for me, once I leave my rally with the voters; I have to spend an hour at the office. You'll be OK?"

"Yes, Mom, I will be. Soon this will be over, however God decides."

"I'm getting pretty excited, think I might have a shot at it."

"I love you, Mom. I'll have decaf ready for you when you get home. I'll be asleep, so I'll say goodnight now."

"I love you, Audra, goodnight."

℘

"There'll be a large crowd. That's why we're getting here early."

Audra held her mom's hand as they entered the large Baptist church in Ephrine. Ashley looked around as the memorial service began.

"I can't believe how many people I know. I really did try to get out and meet the folks who voted for this man in the many elections for which he ran," she thought to herself.

The ceremony celebrated this legislator's life. Many people spoke, offering praise for his efforts over the years. Ashley left the service a little shaken. She and Audra walked to the large reception hall near the church.

"Oh Audra, after everything I heard, whow, do you think I'll ever be able to fill this man's shoes?"

"Absolutely, Mom, don't dwell on what all those folks spoke about. He was all about the 20th century. But Mom, you're a newbie, a younger woman, from the 21st century, with all the ideas that need to be implemented here and now. Go to it Mom, I'll be around. Make your rounds and talk to the folks who'll be voting for you."

Audra watched her mom smile to her. She squeezed her mom's hand and walked away. Audra kept smiling the whole time she was there and talked with several volunteers in her mom's campaign who came to the funeral and reception out of respect for the representative's family.

"Your mom, she's gonna do great."

Audra turned to see Grant standing near her.

She smiled, "I thought that voice sounded familiar."

"Once she gets elected," Grant began.

"Stop, let's not get ahead of ourselves, sonny," Audra said in her best older-lady crackly voice.

Grant laughed, at the sounds, "Gotta ask, are you and your mom interviewing any students about living with you spring semester, while your mom's away?"

Audra put her hand to her forehand, "And you're a mind reader, besides," she giggled.

She nodded to him.

"Yeah, in progress, that's good. I've enjoyed working with your mom so much. I've about half decided to study up for the LSAT. Yeah, I know, I know, I'm just about to finish a masters. But, I got that itch, to help others."

"Your student debt?" Audra nodded as she raised her eyebrows and looked up to him, "what about that?"

"That's the stumbling block. Take care, Audra, we'll see each other, one of these days, in celebration."

She watched him walk away and greet folks that he knew from working her mom's campaign. She continued to move around through the reception crowd and found her way to the food area. Besides coffee she held a piece of cheese cake. Audra found a corner and drank the tasty coffee and downed the cheese cake. After she disposed of the cup and plate, she got up and went to folks who volunteered for her mom. She introduced herself, proud that she could remember so many names. And she felt happy that these folks came to honor this man who helped her state of Georgia.

ℂ

Their minister stopped by on that Sunday morning in November as Audra practiced with her young singers. He listened to the pure melodic sounds of little children singing a cappella.

Audra clapped and Reverend Hailey joined in after they completed the final song of the practice.

"Audra, I need your help."

He stood near her as the children left the choir room to join their parents for the service. She waited as he began, not liking the sour look on his usually pleasant face. He shook his head to her.

"Mrs. Dalter called yesterday. She's in charge of the Christmas program for the Christmas Eve service. She can't do it, says there're family issues. So be it, I have to find someone else."

Audra counted out in her head the number of weeks until Christmas. Then she spoke, "You'd like me to take over?"

She watched him look at her with disbelieving eyes as he nodded and smiled, "I think you're reading my thoughts, uh let me explain."

He went over what little he knew about the plan.

"Essentially you want something of Christ's birth, at the manger?" Audra asked.

"Yes, like that."

"Just so happens I'm doing a paper in English class about someone I admire. I picked St. Francis of Assisi, a truly inspiring man, a saint."

She explained in several sentences what St. Francis began.

"Let's see a script, sounds like that's something we can go with."

"So I'll essentially take sections of my paper, *The Manger, It's Beginning*, and write out the narration and the few lines that the actors will speak. I'll want a narrator, he's critical, as he speaks the most. OK if I have a narrator in the manger scene?"

Reverend nodded his head, "I don't see why not; I'll be curious to see what you come up with."

Two days later Audra dropped the script off to reverend. He called her late that afternoon as she finished her voice and piano practicing.

"I like it, let's do it. I'm putting a piece in the bulletin about this for Christmas Eve. I'll ask for volunteers to play the parts; as they contact me I'll forward their names and phone numbers to you. Let me write down the folks you need."

"Yes, please, so either young people or adults will play the parts. There'll be: the narrator, Mary and a baby doll, Joseph, two shepherds, five people, including a child, St. Francis and one of his brothers (from his religious order) to help perform. Everyone will wear regular clothes; the one exception is that all will have veils or coverings for their heads, hats/caps for the men. Also, please indicate in your piece that we'll practice for 20 minutes, after the 10:30 service, starting with next Sunday. That'll give us five practices, all we'll really need. I'll work with the narrator, who has the biggest part."

"Thank you Audra, I don't know what we'll do next year, how we'll handle the music, when you're away at school."

"Someone will step up, Reverend, they always do. Oh, there won't be any staging, just small sturdy chairs for Mary and Joseph to sit on. Everyone else will stand around the couple, with Baby Jesus in a basket to represent the manger. It'll be just a 10 minute performance, max."

After church the next Sunday Audra's group stood around her.

She smiled as she gave eye contact to each member of the group, "Thank you everyone for volunteering for this Christmas Eve effort."

She handed out the small booklets the church secretary fixed up for each actor.

"It's just 20 minutes of practice each Sunday, I promise, 'cause you have Sunday dinners and other commitments."

The group clapped, helping Audra lighten up the practice mood.

"A strong projecting voice, for the narrator, let me hear your voice."

"That'd be me," a tall man spoke out.

Audra nodded, and everyone clapped. She quickly cast the rest of the play as volunteers stepped forward.

"We'll all learn about early times, in the company of St. Francis, his brother and the folks around the manger."

The last five minutes Audra gave the cast directions, most actors coming down the church aisle, while Mary and Joseph sat in the church sanctuary.

"Good job," she told them all as she concluded the practice. "We'll definitely be ready."

"A history lesson about the manger scene," one cast member commented.

"See you next week, right after the service."

"Thank you, Audra, you really know how to direct us."

They clapped for her.

"Yeah, I been doing this kind of stuff for many years."

One man spoke out, "We can tell."

The group laughed, as Audra joined in, laughing at herself.

As the group began to disperse, Isabella came up to Audra.

She smiled to her, each of them with their shining very dark eyes.

"Thank you for casting me as Mary; you could not know this but I've always wanted to play Mary in some kind of a Christmas production. But, being black, I just never thought it could happen. This is perfect!"

Audra patted Isabella's shoulder, "I'm so glad; I did not know you ever wanted to be an actor, beings you've always danced."

They hugged, and Isabella left, smiling back to Audra as she walked toward the back of the church.

Reverend joined her near the sanctuary.

"How'd it go? I stood in the back, out of the way, you certainly know what you're doing."

"I thought it went very well for first practice, Reverend, we'll be ready. It's always important to keep it simple."

ℰℴ

Audra held tight to her mom. She turned and watched the happy look on her mom's face. Ashley took Audra's left hand and raised it up above their heads with her right arm.

"143, 143, 143, 143, 143," the crowd shouted out as they clapped their hands. Audra heard the click click and felt the bright lights of many cameras. Grant stood away from them, talking to three different reporters. It was late and Audra had school the next day. Earlier in the evening Ben stopped by the campaign headquarters with encouraging words as the vote counting went on. Now she nodded to her mom and found her way to the back office. With coat and purse she headed home in her own car. She knew there would be champagne and congratulations all around for her mom.

"Dad," she heaved a big sigh as she drove, "Aren't you so proud of mom, I am and I wish you could be here in person. Your spirit shines upon us, just like God's does."

Ashley invited her whole campaign group to enjoy food and coffee or pop on the Saturday night after the Tuesday election. Audra helped her mom with the food as the caterers brought it in. They spread the delicious-smelling trays out over a large portion of the kitchen island.

"I haven't done much of this kind of stuff, Audra."

Audra hugged her mom, "You're doing fine, Mom, I want you to relax and enjoy this time with your folks. They appreciate and care about you. They voted for you, in anticipation of policies you may be able to help accomplish for our state."

Everyone ate and talked and laughed about oddities in this campaign Ashley won. She took a few minutes half way through the celebration to thank everyone.

"And Grant, well, he was truly my right hand man. You may not know it, but he took half a day Thursday, from his studies, to return the little office where we all did so much good work, well, he cleaned it up, the windows, even that bathroom."

Someone spoke up, "Well, that was one well used bathroom."

Everyone laughed and turned to Grant and clapped.

"I went in on Friday, after he asked me to stop by the campaign office to pick up several posters I wanted. Gosh, I teared up when I saw it all cleaned up. And the posters, I got them, thanks, Grant. To let you know, I have my paper about all your activities with us, I'll e-mail it to your advisor tomorrow. What an effort, my grateful thanks."

She smiled to Grant and patted her hand over her heart.

Several guests stayed on past seven when the party ended. They spoke with Ashley in the great room as Audra cleaned up. There were two things her mom wanted to remind her of, keys and phones. Once the guests left Audra brought her mom a cup of decaf coffee at the empty kitchen island.

"All cleaned up, Mom, thank goodness for disposable trays, plates, cups, silverware. Almost all the food gone, gosh, they like to eat."

"Thanks, Audra, for the coffee, for the evening, for everything you've done to help me this whole fall. I certainly knew your dad was here."

"Oh, Mom, me too, his presence, inside us, and outside, like I've said before, he rides upon the clouds."

Audra stopped and then remembered, "Somethin' you were supposed to ask me to remind you of."

"Course, the keys, which I'll return to the landlord on Monday. The phones shut off today, and I have them in the trunk for returning. Grant's kept up the budget situation. We ended up in the hole, by about $28, which I paid up myself. But all the donations, down to the penny, donor's name, address, phone number, are available, in case the officials ever ask."

"Wow, Mom, now we'll interview the two students interested in living here for spring and watching over me."

"That's right, that's to be done. After church tomorrow, Audra, I gotta go to the office. It'll be a late night there. I'm super behind. You'll be OK?"

"Absolutely."

"How's stuff for church, Christmas Eve, your manger scene?"

"All set up, and my kid's choir, they'll sing during the offering of the service on Christmas Eve. Grandpa Clint and Grandma Brenda seem eager to visit us this holiday. They'll get to see my church efforts and talk to you."

"Well, Audra, I'm more than just a small city lawyer and a mom."

She hugged her mom, "I don't want to be a smarty ass, but you've taken a few steps up the admiration ladder, and my grandparents sure know it."

"Your Granddad and Grandma Tsosie, they're sure super proud of me."

Ashley nodded to her daughter, tears forming in her eyes.

"Awesome, Mom."

&

"I'm eating fast; if you can, meet me in the library for the last 15 minutes of lunch. I got news."

"And so do I."

Audra watched Ben's smile as he moved toward her with his long-legged stride. They sat together at a table in the back of the library.

Audra nodded.

"It's Auburn."

"Right."

She shook her head to him, a questioning look in her dark eyes.

"I know, I never said for sure, it's Notre Dame."

"Really?"

Ben watched Audra's surprised look, her forehead furrowed and her eyes wide.

"Yeah, my folks're alums. They're happy."

"Are you?"

"Not sure, I've been having fun, in my actor, dance, singing world. Now I gotta face the real world."

"You're awesome in math, already aced your accounting class, that'd be a natural for you."

"I dunno, Audra."

She watched his eyes, darkening to a deep blue, worry sparking in them."I'm startin' to feel way outa my comfort zone."

She nodded to him, "I'm not gonna leave my comfort zone, Ben. I gotta turn in my admissions paperwork to the Music Education program. Then I'll have my auditions in February. I sure won't make a lot of money, but if this all works, I'll be doin' what I love. And kids, well, they're who I want to be with."

They rose together and hugged.

"I want so bad to kiss you, Ben."

"I want your kiss, too," he smiled to her.

They walked together until the halls separated for where they needed to go.

4

Christmas 2007-Senior Year

"Been awhile, doesn't seem possible, you two, Ashley and Audra, are just as beautiful as the last time I saw you, separate and together," Grandpa Clint said in his quiet Southern drawl. The four of them sat together for the noon Christmas meal.

"You did all this, Audra?" her grandma asked.

"Right, with just a little guidance from mom."

Audra thought the tasty ham, soft scalloped potatoes, salad, rolls, and a small veggie tray made a perfect meal. She asked again this year for red velvet cupcakes for her birthday dessert. Grandma lit the candle on her cupcake before Audra made a wish.

"I really enjoyed the manger scene, Audra, that you produced from a paper you wrote in one of your classes. You even mentioned checking several sources to make certain about St. Francis and what he accomplished," Grandma Brenda spoke out.

"What I liked, Audra, your narrator, his voice, so excellent, how he shared about God becoming one of us, through the folks seeing, experiencing how the Christ Child lay on the hay in a manger. It blew me away that it was St

Francis, back in 1223, in Greccio, Italy. And that he felt it was so important that people see the manger scene. From what I gather from the story the narrator told, St. Francis was really the first person to have the reenactment of the manger scene, wow after all those years. I, for sure, was filled with joy from watching Mary, Joseph, Baby Jesus, and the folks that stood near them."

"Grandpa Clint, can you even imagine what other feelings the original folks had who gathered with St. Francis and his brothers?"

"I can't, just in awe, I think of what they were watching."

"Audra, to this day, the reenactment of the manger scene, the Christ Child and His humble birth, is such a part of the Christmas experience for mankind," Ashley murmured to them, "joy to the world."

They all nodded.

Later that afternoon Audra performed for her mom and grandparents. As she explained, this was a practice for her auditions at Auburn in February. She performed the two voice and two piano songs. She accompanied herself on the voice selections. After that she demonstrated several of the scales and arpeggios she would perform on the piano, and the scales she would sing for voice.

"I'll have an accompanist for my voice. The administrator of each of my auditions will finally ask me to sight read a piece. That's what scares me the most. So I pick two pieces every day, often things I haven't seen before in my piano and voice books, and I sight read them. Grandma, would you please pick two pieces for me to sight read?"

Brenda found one voice and one piano piece that didn't look too difficult to her, and asked Audra to sing and play. When Audra finished, she turned and smiled to her family.

They clapped and all three of them came to her as she stood by the piano.

"Group hug, yes!"

"Thank you for listening to me and your enthusiasm, and those two summer camps you gave me, the confidence, they helped so much," Audra shared as they hugged.

Before they drove away the next morning her grandparents let Audra know how pleased they were that she got admitted to Auburn, her dad's school.

"You're called a legacy, that means a parent attended the school," Grandma Brenda informed Audra.

"Did you know," Ashley spoke up, "that Abby also plans to attend Auburn, been admitted? So Audra and Abby may get to know each other better as collegiates."

"No, we didn't know. You young ladies will not be far from us in Montgomery. We'll have to have you over for weekend visits and meals."

Clint and Brenda also shared with Ashley as they finished breakfast the next morning, "We're gosh awful proud of you, your election to the Georgia House. And we know you'll have your hands full with all the legislation coming up."

She nodded to Audra and her in-laws.

"I certainly will have. I'll really only do early breakfast in the tiny apartment I rented near the capitol. But the furnished studio is perfect for me; I'll spend only sleep time in it and take lunches and dinners at the capitol or near it. Course, I'll come home as many weekends as I can, when the committees don't run over into the weekend."

As they walked out to her grandparents' car, her grandpa told her how much they enjoyed hearing Audra's kids a cappella choir during the Christmas Eve service.

"I will miss the kids."

As she turned to hug her grandpa, he whispered in her ear, "Just the beginning, of all the young people who'll sing with you, sooner than you think."

She stepped back away from him and gave him her wide smile, nodding. She moved to the passenger side of the car, hugging her grandma.

"We'll see you, it'll be very soon, your graduation, unbelievable, Audra, thank you for this wonderful time with you and your mom."

She nodded and moved next to Ashley. They waved as the grandparents drove away.

"Audra, that went very well; thanks again for being such a lovely hostess. It was, well, a super Christmas. Brenda and Clint, gosh, things are better for me, with them, that's for sure. And I can't wait to see my folks; oh, they've decided."

"What's that?"

They held hands as they walked up to the front door.

Audra opened the front door for her mom.

"Mom and dad, they're coming for your graduation."

Ashley watched the smile widen on her daughter's face, "Perfect, we'll all be here, our whole family, dad, he'll be looking down, heaping love and hope on all of us."

&

"Is your mom going out tonight for New Year's Eve"?

"Nope, she's staying home, so sad, still in shock, just like we are; she's gonna miss the memorial, has to be in Atlanta, starting day after tomorrow, driving there tomorrow afternoon."

"The session starts that soon?" Isabella asked.

"Uh huh, lots of preliminary stuff."

The teens got up from sitting on the rug in the basement great room.

"Do you remember this routine?" Sophia asked as she and Isabella began.

"Yeah, embedded in my brain, forever. Jeffy, this is for you."

As Audra danced around the room with her friends, her thought went to her dad, "You're not alone now, Jeff's mom's up there with you, up in the sky, riding the clouds."

Audra felt salty tears scour her eyes. As they finished the routine, she held out her arms. Sophia and Isabella saw her tears. They came into the hug and they all broke down, crying and crying.

Audra found tissues and they sat back down together.

"Everybody needs to talk. Sophia, you start."

"What now, I asked myself, and still do, how do we go on? Our friend, Jeff, he's hurtin' so bad."

"Guys," Audra blew her nose and took in deep breaths, "what I did when my dad died; you put one foot in front of the other. You get up every morning and go on. Time, that's what'll help most. And remember, God blesses us, every day. Be grateful, we got so much."

"How can a mom, how can anybody drink so much that you wander outside in a snowstorm, slip and fall down in a snowdrift at a Stowe VT ski resort, pass out, and die of hypothermia?"

"Can't fathom that, and unbelievable, a prof at Humphrey University. Isn't Jeff's dad also a professor?"

"Right, he is. Jeff looked so forward to skiing with his folks and sister. It was to be a skiing Christmas for them." Audra paused, shaking her head as she sought words to speak, "Guys, there's somethin' I can tell you now, a secret in Jeff's family. But he shared with me, when he finally could. Dr. Alicot was an alcoholic, tried AA and several other treatment programs. Nothing seemed to help her. I suggested several times that Jeff go to Alateen; I'd go with him. He refused, wanted to continue to hide his mom's stuff from everyone he knew, like nothing was going on. He never accepted that his mom suffered from an illness."

"Like your dad, with the brain tumor, I guess that's acceptable, but alcoholism, like people think it's something that can be fixed. But it can't," Sophia broke into tears again.

"Has anyone heard from Jeff?"

The girls shook their heads.

"Mom told me her law firm is handling the estate, and she's had a chance to talk to Jeff's dad. She says he's completely devastated, so are Jeff and his sister. There can be lots of denial in the family of an alcoholic."

"Should we be trying to reach out to Jeff?"

The teens locked their eyes on Audra's.

"Mom suggested we wait until after we attend his mom's memorial service the day after New Year's."

"That makes sense," Isabella replied.

"Oh, Jeff's dad asked my mom if I'd be with Jeff for the memorial and the reception after at the Alicot home."

"You'll do it, right Audra?"

"Course, Jeff is my dear friend. He was with me, for everything for dad."

"The stuff for Jeff's mom, sounds like it'll be a lot like what you and your mom did for your dad, except more subdued."

"Yeah, I think so; Jeff shared with his folks as he went through mourning with me. I remember that his parents came to the celebration at our house."

"Oh Audra, there were so many people who came and went at your dad's celebration. I remember lots of food, people chatting and there was some laughter, your dad's favorite songs in the background. It was the first time we met your grandparents. And then we got to meet your other grandparents a little later. Now we know who your beautiful mom resembles," Isabella nodded as she smiled to Audra.

"You'll be coming to Jeff's?"

"Uh huh, but we're only coming to the reception with our parents. So we'll see you there. Be brave, Audra."

The three girls hugged and ran upstairs. They smelled the popcorn Ashley fixed for them. Isabella asked Ashley to join them in a card game until 11:30 when they turned on television to get ready for the ball drop in NYC. The four of them sat on the couch, toasting each other with glasses of sparkling cider.

"Our lives are gonna change so much, in this New Year," Sophia sat forward, turning as she eyed the other three.

"To 2008," four voices spoke up.

ℬ

Audra helped carry the final bags Ashley wanted on the front seat passenger side of her sedan. She walked back in the house behind Audra.

"I need to say goodbye to Saila."

Ashley went upstairs, surveyed her neat and clean bedroom and bathroom and headed down the hall to the graduate student's room. She knocked on the partially closed door.

Saila opened the door and asked her in.

"Just about moved in, this is a super room for me, and so nice to have a parking spot in your garage. It'll be a great semester for me, for Audra, and I know you'll do great in the legislature."

"Thanks, Saila, I'm somewhat frightened by all the newness I'll face."

"It'll be an awesome challenge. And I will watch over your daughter. She's got so much going on; the audition being number one in her world. We'll be fine. Please just concentrate your efforts on the state of things in Georgia."

They hugged. As Ashley left the room, she felt a sense of peace, of well being come over her.

"Will, is that you, or God, or maybe both of you?" she questioned as she and Audra held hands, moving to her car.

Mother and daughter hugged.

"Mom, good luck, God speed."

"I love you."

"And I love you."

Audra watched as her mom drove away.

"I wonder if this is how mom'll feel next fall as she sees me drive away to Auburn? I feel like a mom sending a kidlet off to school," she giggled.

Once inside her home she added, "'cept what she'll do is much more challenging than studying at a university, making decisions that will affect everyone in the state of Georgia."

$\wp$

"You gotta step up, Audra," she told herself. "Jeff stood by me all the time with dad."

At the appointed time she got ready to join Jeff at his home.

"I'm glad I listened to the weather forecast. It's gonna be a freezing cold and windy time at the grave site. I'll be bundled up with a warm hat on my head."

As she drove to his home, she looked out to see the sun peeking out from the gray morning clouds.

"Dad, are you up there, riding the clouds?" she questioned.

The family went to the cemetery in a limousine provided by the mortuary. Only a few very close friends and family were invited to the service. Jeff clutched Audra's hand the whole way to Pine View. The minister spoke in brief terms about Dr. Alicot. The five minute remembrance ended with everyone joining in for *The Lord's Prayer*. Each participant placed a white rose at the small wooden box where Jeff's mom's ashes reposed. From there the group reassembled at the Alicot home where many more folks stopped by to visit with the family. People enjoyed spicy Mexican and Italian finger foods, veggie trays, cupcakes of various flavors, coffee, tea, and punch. Audra heard ABBA's songs in the background. She teared up as she remembered how Jeff and his mom used to whirl around in the living room with Audra, dancing to the lively songs from that rock group.

"Stay close to me, Audra," Jeff whispered to her, "you're my rock right now."

Audra touched the shoulder of his suit jacket as she looked into his sad, far away eyes.

"As you were for me, I'm here, Jeffy."

For the next hour and a half they moved around in the Alicot great room and kitchen, talking to guests. Jeff introduced Audra as his best friend. Sophia and Isabella each came with their parents. After visiting with the six of them

Audra actually saw Jeff give the families a small smile. They broke away from the visitors twice to have a snack. Jeff had punch. Audra drank the tasty hazelnut coffee.

"I bet they used the same caterers we've used, knowing Jeff, he knew every detail from our celebration reception," Audra thought. "And another thing, this home looks so cleaned up; that musta been Jeannie, Jeff's big sis."

She decided to ask Jeff. When she did, he pulled her to a quiet area.

"About that, Audra, dad asked us to slick everything up; mom was no housekeeper, especially after Jeannie left for college."

"Sheesh, Jeff, she worked, taught night as well as day classes, paper grading, tests, prep for lectures."

"You're right," he paused as she watched his blue eyes darken, "I'm just super angry right now. And oh my gosh, as we detrashed the house, we found 15 bottles of various kinds of booze, hidden, can you believe it?"

"Yeah, I can. She had a very serious illness."

"So, my sis and me, we took all the bottles out to a far back dirt area covered in pine straw, and we dumped out every bottle of liquor. Sure as heck we didn't want that going into the sewer, and, ick, maybe back in our drinking water. We've yet to decide whether we'll tell dad."

"How's he doing?"

"Right," Jeff paused, "now he goes to Alanon every chance he gets, but school starts at the university soon for him. He looks good, like a great huge weight's been lifted from his mind. I've even seen him smile a couple of times. Best of all, he's going to the gym, real early. Getting exercise is the best. He's having an awful time sleeping, like we all are. All of us're having nightmares. But we're in grief counseling. Jeannie's classes start next week so she's gotta head out. She's been a huge help."

"You got the cooking, laundry, and housework under control?"

"Yeah, Audra, you've taught me so much, about going on after a loss."

"Hey Jeff, you know I can help you."

He nodded to her, unsmiling. Audra stayed on after all the guests left, including the few family members who drove or flew in. She helped Jeff and Jeannie clean up the kitchen area and the great room. Again, she could not believe how nice the whole home looked. And another thing surprised her.

"Why had I not seen this before; Jeff's in a big growth spurt. Gosh, he's taller than I am by several inches. When did that happen?"

She found Jeannie, "I'll have to go; you've done an awesome job with all this."

"Yeah, I'm exhausted, but I'm feeling less angry; it's time, each day removed from her death, it gets better. Dad's deal now is removing everything from her office at the university, a big job since she taught for many years. Mom's replacement is moving in very soon to that office. Let me hug you, dear Audra. You've grown up so much since I saw you last. Thank you for being here for my bro."

They hugged. Audra found Jeff and his dad in the large sunroom in the back part of the first floor.

Jeff's dad stood with his son. He came forward and hugged Audra. They stepped back from each other.

"Thank you Audra, I still pray for your dad, every day, as I now pray for Jeff's mother."

"Same, sir."

Jeff and Audra held hands until they found her things in an upper guest bedroom. He helped her on with her coat, and she let him put on her hat, plunk, on top of her head.

"Thank you, Audra, God bless and keep you. I love you."

Audra looked into his blue eyes and touched his cheek with her hand, "God bless you. I love you, Jeff."

She could feel his eyes on her as she walked down the steps and away from the Alicot home. Tears streamed so hard from her eyes that she almost stumbled on a crack in the sidewalk.   She walked several blocks to her car.   After spending five minutes praying she drove, headed for home, thinking of her dad, aching from how much she missed him.

℘

Weeks went by for Audra. The grinding hard work equaled practicing, doing homework, housework, laundry, and keeping herself fed. She caught a cold and lost her voice two and a half weeks before her February audition at Auburn. That weekend Ashley came home and ordered Audra to bed until she felt better. Before Ashley left Sunday afternoon, Audra declared she needed to go to school the next day.

"Mom, I hated missing choir practice with my little kids, and Senior Sing."

"It was necessary, this week, do you get it, your voice?"

"I do, Mom, I realize I'm not indestructible."

"Jeff's really worried about you; so's Ben. I've talked to both of them. They understand about your voice. So I've been your vocal cords."

Ashley headed back to Atlanta after she kissed Audra in her room.

"Don't get off your bed now, lots of liquids down that throat. Saila's taking your temp in the morning. If it's OK, you'll go to school. She's standing in for the doc, OK?"

Audra nodded to her mom, closed her eyes and rested until she fell asleep. Her voice returned, a little each day. She did her voice practice in her head, recalling each note and lyric.

"It's taking me longer to get my homework back under control. I guess I've been pretty sick," she told herself.

℘

"God help me through this day," Audra prayed the morning of her auditions.

By the end of the day, she thanked God for all the wondrous gifts He bestowed upon her. She accomplished what she set out to do nearly a year ago. Both her Auburn audition administrators, voice and piano, complimented her on her efforts.

"I'll know by the end of February, if I made it into the music education program," she said as she sat with her mom and Grandma Brenda at the hotel restaurant on the Friday morning after the Thursday audition.

Her grandma called the week before.

"I'd like to come and have breakfast with you and your mom, before you return to Ephrine on Friday. I'll get up early and drive from Montgomery to Auburn, it's really just a short hop."

Audra realized how much her grandma really cared for her, to make that driving effort.

Before the three of them departed, Grandma Brenda hugged Audra.

"We can't wait for your graduation, dear granddaughter."

"Oh, I haven't told you, the community theater director for the spring play called me. I'm standing in for a singer/dancer who's gotten ill. It'll be good for me to have one final experience."

"Don't want to sound like a grandma, but I am," Audra laughed as she heard her grandma giggle, "my dear, you've also got all your practicing for voice and piano you want to continue, plus you're learning the violin and the clarinet. And you've got your home to care for, and homework, your mom, still in Atlanta, will you be OK?"

Audra stood back from her grandma and smiled, "Time management, Grandma, time management. I can do this."

Grandma Brenda held her granddaughter's hand and gave it a little squeeze as she nodded to her. They all said their goodbyes. Audra helped her mom drive back to Ephrine. They arrived home late Friday night.

Before Ashley returned to Atlanta on that Saturday she shared as they finished breakfast.

"Audra, I loved being with you at Auburn. You were so prepared; your maturity level really impresses me. I've much catching up to do from missing sessions on Thursday and Friday. Several members, one in each of my committees, covered for me while I was at Auburn with you."

Audra touched her mom's arm and smiled at her, "Thanks Mom, for taking time away from the legislature, to be with me. I really needed your support."

"My folks, on my committees, they certainly understand; most everyone has kids. They wanted you to do really well, which you have."

"Sounds like you all root for your children."

"We do, like you, all the kids are involved in so many different things, so much talent, like you've got."

Once again, Audra helped her mom bring out her bags for returning to Atlanta. They said their goodbyes. As she saw her mom's car disappear down the street, Audra let out a big breath.

"Oh my goodness, let me get the calendar and plan out the rest of my time until school's out."

After she made another pot of coffee and put the dishes in the dishwasher, she took the calendar from its place next to the kitchen phone. She sat down at the kitchen island and plotted out her activities until June. Once she got into April she ran up to get her notes on the dates for the community play. She took several drinks of her coffee and finished up the months of April and May. She went back and put a big star next to the end of February date.

"Gosh," she shook her head, "it won't be that long before I'll know if I'm in the ME program."

&

Audra waited in her car for Jeff. When he did get in, Audra told him how upset she was with him.

"We're gonna be late for Alateen. You know I hate walking in late."

"Yeah, I know Audra, here's the deal; this is my last time going. It isn't helping me right now. I need that time for homework."

They talked as Audra drove Jeff home.

"When you're in the meeting, are you paying attention or worrying about stuff?"

"Yup, that's exactly right. I'm having a really hard time concentrating on anything. So I worry, and no, I'm not paying attention. When'll this get better?"

"Time, Jeff, you just gotta plow through the days, try to thank God for each day. You're still going to grief counseling with your dad?"

"I am, it's the most time I've spent with my dad in many years."

"Hey, that sounds good for both of you."

"Yeah, it is. And Audra, thank you for being with me. I know you got play practice, homework plus learning your instruments, and running your home. Aren't you exhausted?"

"Once was, but it's time management, I tell folks, like I learned in Girl Scouts. I don't fix anything fancy to eat for myself. Saila fixes her own. I save most of the cooking for the weekends that mom comes home. And mom helps."

She drove to the front of his house. He leaned across and kissed her cheek.

"I love you, my forever friend."

"Same," she turned to him and gave him a small smile.

℃

"Mom, I'm in. My future, I know, I feel confident, I'm happy."

"Audra, that's fabulous news. You did so well in your auditions; I had a good feeling. I won't be home this weekend; too many things hanging over and we've got an all-day legislative session in the House for Saturday."

"Think the legislature, both houses, will be able to finish up by the end of March?"

"Looks doubtful, once in a while we run into April by a couple of days. That may be the case this time."

"You do what you have to do. Crazy here, *Ships Ahoy* is well into production. I really like what I'm doing, the singing and dancing, in the background, not the pressure of a lead like with Fiona and Elaine in past plays. I hope you'll get to see it, a fun musical."

"Is Ben participating?"

"Nope, wanted to do track, his last chance. He knows he's not a good enough trackster for collegiate. And I'm working on a special song. I'll tell you more when I see you next, Mom."

"I'm looking forward to it, love you, Audra."

"I love you, Mom."

The song worked in her head as she hung up the phone. She grabbed paper and went to the grand piano, writing down notes as she played, and words to the song after she got the melody finished. The melody came to her as she drove away from Jeff the last night they went together to Alateen. Once she got the chord notes written down on a lined musical score and added the lyrics, she let Ben know what her plan was.

That night before play practice she pulled Ben aside to a piano not being used in the back of the Ephrine city auditorium. He wanted to come to the play practice to see Audra, and how the production moved along. She sat down, played the notes and sang. He listened to her full alto voice and the accompanying words. The second time through the piece Ben joined his voice with Audra's.

"My thought is that our a cappella group should perform this at commencement. They're so many seniors in the group; yeah, we wanta do a special thing." She turned and looked up to Ben. "Somethin's missing, I think it's in the lyrics. Here's a copy for you and I'd like you to consider the words. I'm gonna propose it to the graduation committee. I'm one of the seniors asked to help out with the graduation ceremony, the planning."

"OK, I'll see what I can do; that's a great idea, Audra, to my knowledge that group hasn't performed for a graduation."

"Yeah, that's why I'm gonna ask. But the song's got to be just right, for the ceremony. Thanks, Ben, you're so good at this kind of stuff. I can do the music, but the words, not so much."

Ben watched the production, this being one of the last practices before the final dress rehearsal. She joined him where he sat afterward, middle level, in the auditorium.

"Whatcha think?"

"It's good; I'm not the director, so I try to go with the flow of the show. You, and all the other singer/dancers, do a really good job. I hope it's fun for you, the performing," his blue eyes joined to her brown ones as they sat together.

"Yeah, it'll be my last play, for awhile. It's just that when I get home, I still got homework, and practice."

"Have you thought about getting up early?"

"I do, 5 in the morning, I turn on the coffee and practice my clarinet and violin in the basement. That way I don't disturb Saila."

"Audra," he turned toward her, "Please, will you come to Prom with me?"

She gazed into his eyes, her mind scattering over all the dances in her past. She took her time, then smiled and nodded, "I accept. I've been, but just in a group, to prom. This is special, with you, our last big school dance together, of our high school lives."

"Thanks, I like dancing with you so much; you're so fluid and light in my arms."

They hugged. Audra handed him one of her bags as they stood up. She carried the other one as they held hands.

"Ben, please don't walk me up, I'm totally exhausted," she told him as he stopped his car in front of Audra's home. They reached across and hugged each other.

"Got it, sleep tight, babe, 5 comes early."

"Thanks for understanding."

Ben waited until Audra got in her home; she turned and waved to him.

"Let me figure out other words to this song, Audra," he spoke out as he drove home. "It's a nice melody, kinda reminds me of the lyrics in a song about we've only just begun. That, for sure, is us as we graduate; we're starting over, the beginning of the next stage of our lives."

℘

Ships Ahoy completed Audra's drama career for her high school days. Ashley got three DVD's of the production and sent one to each of Audra's grandparents.

"I'll see them soon, Mom, it's so nice they have one final look at this time of my life. Gosh, I got a small library of all my efforts."

"That you can enjoy, play back, for the rest of your life."

"And maybe show my own students, someday."

Audra hugged her mom as they stood together in the kitchen.

"Glad you're finished, I'm happy to have you home."

"Oh, Dra, I've a law project that I gotta finish up for my firm. I'll be in Atlanta just a little bit more."

"Another week?"

"Yes, just a part of it, I want to be home for your prom, graduation, the families coming, so I'll get 'er done now."

Her mom had three more days left in Atlanta. Audra enjoyed having her evenings available for homework and instrument practice, without the play production.

"Audra."

"Hey, Jeff, you haven't called for awhile."

"I know, stuff happening. I need your help. It's dad."

"Want me to come over, uh, right now?"

"Yeah, please ask Saila to come with you. She's 21, right?"

"'Course."

On the way over to the Alicot home Audra filled Saila in on much that she knew about Jeff's situation. Jeff let them in after they tapped on the front door.

Jeff hugged Audra and shook Saila's hand. Audra heard loud music coming from the sunroom in the back of the home. He pointed his dad out to them. He seemed to be asleep on the sofa. Jeff turned the music down and waved them away from the room and toward the front of the home. They sat together on a couch in the great room.

"Dad, dad," Jeff put his head in his hands and sobbed, "he's been like this every week night for the last three weeks."

Audra's gut fired up as her tears began, a wrenching sadness smacking her like a slap across the face.

She touched Jeff's cheek, "Look at me, Jeff, I can smell it, he's drunk, passed out, right?"

"Your sister know?" Saila asked.

Jeff directed his gaze at Audra, "She does."

"Hey, isn't your dad teaching this semester?"

"He's on a one semester sabbatical, working with tax CPA's on a special project. So he goes in once in a while, but not teaching students or advising."

"Gosh, I'm not clear, what's a sabbatical?"

"Audra, after a professor's been at a university for a period of time, they are allowed time off to work on special research projects, stuff like that," Saila added.

"Paid?"

"Yeah, Audra, he's getting paid his regular salary."

"Even though he's not teaching?"

Audra's eyebrows raised and her forehead furrowed as she looked at Saila.

She nodded, "That's correct, it's a special thing a university does for a faculty member who's been there long term. You're heard of the phrase, 'Publish or perish?'"

"Uh, I guess."

"So Jeff's dad does research, so he can write papers and get his name out among the people in his profession."

The three of them sat together, listening to the soft music from the back. Audra's thoughts slogged around in her head like mushy oatmeal.

"What now, Jeff?" She turned, her eyes questioning him.

"Jeannie and I've talked. She's getting him into a 6-week rehab program, one of the programs moms tried, but didn't work, and she dropped out."

"Is he gonna wake up?"

"Not until morning, I cover him with a blanket, sometimes he rolls off the couch so I move everything away so he doesn't hurt himself."

"Oh my gosh, what's happened, Jeff?"

Audra began to tear up as he looked at her with his sad eyes.

"He's not handling mom's death, at all. He's stopped Alanon and the exercising. Hey, I don't think he's alcoholic, just needs stuff to numb the pain of his loss. Like with him, my sis, me, we feel responsible for what happened to mom."

"Your mom, she had an illness."

"Yeah, I know, that statement only helps me part of the time."

"What can we do to help you, Jeff? I asked you that a lot, after her death."

Audra watched Jeff raise his eyes to her. He shook his head as his tears began again. Saila took Audra by the shoulder, and they left the room for a little while. The two of them spoke in whispers. Audra nodded her head and smiled to Saila.

They returned. Audra sat down next to Jeff and patted his arm. Saila stood next to the couch, beside Audra.

"For the time that your dad is away for rehab, that six weeks, I would really like you to come and live with mom, Saila, and me. In our basement there's a couch that makes into a bed, and there's a full bathroom down there."

"Oh my gosh, Audra, that's my huge worry, will I get sent to foster care?"

"Jeff, I think not, if we can get this arranged," Saila nodded her head. "You are still a minor, but you're getting close to being of legal age; you're getting close to graduation. When're you and your sis thinking of committing him?"

"This weekend, like he sobers up and doesn't drink on Saturday and Sunday. He goes to church on Sunday. And he stays after for the snacks and coffee with his fellow church goers. He really seems to like that."

Jeff shifted his eyes from Audra to Saila and back to Audra, "They don't know everything that goes on, and they don't judge, God's helpers."

Audra remained silent for a little while, "Two things, Jeff, where's all the stuff from your mom's office at the university?"

"Dumpster at the university, Dad threw everything away. Mom had a small area in the sunroom, that stuff's all tossed."

"OK," Saila nodded, "I've been thinking, since I'm a grad student, what about the time left on your dad's sabbatical? Is he going to have time to do all the research he needs to help out the tax CPA's?"

Jeff sat back and thought for a moment.

"Yeah, dad's lovin' this project, did so much research on it after fall semester ended. He really didn't want to go on the ski vacation with us, wanted to stay and do research. Then all of a sudden he decided the trip was important. I'm sure he's glad he went."

"How so?"

"We got two ski days together, my folks and Jeannie and me. It's a time I'll never forget. We, we," he stopped, "such a great time."

Jeff's tears began again.

"So, do you think he'll be able to finish the project and his paper by the time his sabbatical is over, that'll be in late May?"

Jeff remained quiet, thinking about the question and wiping his eyes, "Yeah, hope so, hey, when the program he's going into gets him sobered up, I think he'll work really hard on his project. He's so lucky, that he's not teaching. We'll make sure he takes everything he needs to write his paper."

Audra touched Jeff's shoulder, "God works in wondrous ways."

ﻌ

With Ashley's legal expertise in matters of medical emergencies, Dr. Sam Alicot got immediate placement in a facility in Macon. Audra heard him say to his family that he really needed help. Jeannie flew from Harvard, rented a car in Atlanta and drove to Ephrine. She and Jeff drove their dad to the facility, Ashton Heights. Within two hours they returned Jeff home to Ephrine. Jeannie returned to Harvard.

"I think Jeff'll be OK alone this one Saturday night in his home. He needs the time to sort out things; he's been a parent to his own dad, for a while. Then we'll move him in with us," Ashley spoke to both Saila and Audra.

The next day after church Audra met Jeff at his home. She stood in front of him in the tidy kitchen as he put his hands over his face and groaned.

"It was pretty awful; dad reduced to terrible shaking from the alcohol withdrawal, and crying pretty nonstop, sheesh Audra, that's after just 3 weeks, what must it be like for those addicted for years, people with delirium tremens?"

She met his tired eyes with her own and just shook her head.

"Gotta try to lighten this mood," she thought. In a perkier voice she spoke up, "You and your sis, your dad will thank you one day."

"Yeah, I know."

"Where are we at with stuff? You stopped the paper?"

"Uh huh."

"Trash?"

"Oh yeah, I got a little bit, which I'll bring to your home, if that's OK?"

"Course, do the neighbors know?"

"Hey, I didn't realize what nice neighbors we have; they're all rooting for dad, for me, for Jeannie, everybody's bein' really positive."

"The mail?"

"I'll stop by three times a week to pick it up; Jeannie was so smart to get me signed up on one of my dad's checking accounts. Oh, and I'll begin watering the perennials in front and back. The yard's been my job for years."

"So you can pay bills?"

"Right."

"Where're your things, Jeff, that you want to take."

"Up in my room, just bringing one suitcase and my backpack. I'll get it."

Audra checked the refrigerator. She smelled the soured milk and poured it out. She found several other items that needed to be removed and taken to the Davisson home as trash. She did a walk through of the rest of the rooms.

"Everything looks good, Jeff," she smiled to him as they started carrying bags to both her and Jeff's cars.

"Heat down?"

"Yeah, where we keep it this time of year, still got the air conditioner off. We'll be using it big time when dad gets home."

"That'll be a joyful time, Jeff, graduation ahead," she stepped to Jeff and they hugged before they got in their cars to move him to Audra's.

℃

"You said you'd wear it up, what happened?"

"I hated the way I looked, made the stylist take it all down and just a few curls on the sides."

"Ben'll be happy; you're a stunner, Audra," Jeff said as he looked her over.

They stood in the Davisson kitchen, Jeff getting ready to leave for his date with Sophia, and Audra waiting for Ben to stop by.

"Don't forget her wrist corsage."

"Oh gosh, I almost did, dude that woulda been so embarrassing."

"See you there."

They hugged and Jeff walked out with Sophia's corsage in his hand.

Audra spotted her mom as she and Ben made their way into the grand ballroom of the hotel. She waved to her. Ashley smiled and waved back. She went early to the dance to help chaperone.

"You're my angel," Ben whispered as they danced close to a quiet romantic song the DJ played.

"And you for sure are my wonderful knight, strong, stalwart, knowing your own mind."

They whirled, and twirled, and turned and twisted to all the different music they danced to that evening. Audra saw her mom dancing to a fast song, turned about by a tall gentleman Audra never saw before. Tears pushed out from the corners of her eyes.

"Oh my gosh, my mom, Ben, my mom."

He turned Audra to where her head indicated and saw Ashley.

"I'm really happy for your mom, Audra," he nodded to her.

"Me too."

Seeing her mom in the company of a man shocked Audra so much that she said very little the rest of the night. She and Jeff danced once, stopping by to see her mom as they finished dancing.

She and Ben sat together with other students at the after prom in the high school cafeteria. They devoured delicious pizza and pop in large quantities. Someone brought a guitar and many joined in the singing. Spur-of-the-moment performances appeared from seniors in the a cappella, chorus, and glee groups. Other students played games. The seniors and their guests pitched in to clean up and the students left, thanking the parents who made the after prom possible.

Ben kissed her at her front door. His soft lips plied hers and they kissed again.

"It shocked you to see your mom with a man, the first time?" he whispered into her ear.

"Uh huh, that I know of. I gotta let go of my mom and dad, hand in hand."

They hugged. As she stepped back he lifted her chin up, "Time, Audra, it'll take time."

She kissed him, "It's already been so long. Oh Ben, tonight was magic, like the magic we created in *Arsenic*."

"Yes, tonight was magic, good night, Audra."

He kissed her on top of her head and turned to leave. She stood at the front door until he returned to his car. She waved, and he waved back. She saw a wide smile on his face.

&

"Jeff's all moved out?" Saila asked as they sat down to dinner together that May night.

"Yeah, I didn't have to fix near as much spaghetti and meat sauce as I've been. I miss his company at dinner these past weeks, so I wanted you to join me."

"Thanks for this nice meal, I super hate to cook."

"I noticed," Audra nodded her head, "I fixed mom a plate for later; she's got a big project that'll keep her at the office. Jeff vacuumed the whole basement and cleaned the entire bathroom. All I have to do is wash up the sheets and towels for company coming for graduation."

Saila touched Audra's arm, "Caution, you've been like a mom to Jeff while his dad's been in rehab. You gotta let go, his dad's home now, the two of them have to make their own way together, or apart. You got too much going on here, Audra, getting ready for finals, graduation, your grandparents coming. And this summer, working and preparing for Auburn, your mom's warned you, you can only be responsible for you."

"I know, I know, it's just that Jeff and I're so close, sometimes I can read his mind, and him mine."

"So I would tell you, since my semester'll be over by then. I think having a graduation party here for both you and Jeff should be your last effort to help him out."

"I got it; he's got to set out on his own."

"Right."

"Saila."

"What, babe?"

"Jeff's talkin' like he's gonna work for a year before he tries to go to school, says his mind is so scattered. He gets all his work done for school, but his heart's not into what's going on. It's kinda the way I sorta drifted along on waves of sadness for awhile after dad left us."

"Hey, I think that's a very good idea for Jeff. He's not ready for the expense and work involved in going to school right now. There's nothing wrong with working for awhile."

"You think so, Saila?"

"Yeah, absolutely."

"Then I'll stop feeling concerned about Jeff's future. Not every kid needs a university education, but they do need advanced training in a particular field. Plumbers and electricians, they do very well for themselves, and we can't survive without them."

"Jeff's got a good head; once he's out in the working world, I think he'll discover the importance of a university education."

"I hope so, 'cause he can't see it now. He just wants to make sure he's OK and his dad's OK."

ॐ

"Balloons, and several signs, Happy Graduation, Best Wishes, that's enough, Mom."

And that's what happened at the Davisson home for the celebration of Audra and Jeff's graduations. Ashley asked that Sam assist, because she knew he couldn't handle a party for Jeff, not now, so newly home from his rehab. The caterers came early and brought in the food and set it out around the kitchen island. What little that needed refrigeration, they took care of it. Audra drove herself to the ceremony. Ashley would bring both sets of grandparents.

Audra heard the rain drumming on the roof of the Ephrine High gymnasium. She looked over and saw Jeff as she and the a cappella group sang the commencement song. With Ben's help on the lyrics the song had everything Audra hoped for. They sang, thanking teachers and parents, remembering special times through high school, the dances, assemblies, sporting events, hard times as students struggled with classes, and good times when students got good grades. At the song's end the singers expressed their gratitude, for the blessings in their lives that brought them to this graduation day. Audra felt her tears come as the song ended. She gazed out at the audience, the graduates in chairs on the gym floor and parents and friends jammed into the bleachers and people standing and sitting to the sides and in the back behind the graduates. Everyone clapped and cheered for the song.

The graduation ceremony usually took place outside, on the football field. Except, this year, like some, the rain brought everyone into a cramped last-minute set up inside. Audra felt a spirit of happiness immerse her, and she hoped, the whole assemblage.

"I'm graduated, hard to believe," Audra thought about that as she greeted fellow students, parents, teachers, and her mom's helpers from the law firm. Several members of her Senior Sing congratulated her. The most moving moments were when her Kids Choir sang her a song. Audra saw their parents standing away from the singers. What really tore at her heart was as they crowded around her after the song. Audra wept, unable to say a word. Applause and laughter came after the little ones sang.

"Please stop crying, Audra", one little singer said, "You'll make us all cry."

She felt her dad, walking along side of her as she moved among the guests in the great room and kitchen. Some folks stood on the covered backyard patio. The rain now was a muggy Georgia mist, not the cool rain at the graduation ceremony.

"Whatcha think, Dad?" she asked as she helped herself to a piece of graduation cake. Jeff wanted carrot, and Audra wanted chocolate, so that's what the cake was, half and half.

"I tried a tiny piece, uuummm, moist, so chocolatey," Audra pointed out to Sophia, who stopped by with Isabella.

"Our graduation isn't for two weeks; Hillyer Academy has nearly three more weeks of classes each year than the public schools."

The teens helped themselves to a small portion of carrot and a small portion of the large sheet cake.

"I'll be there for your graduation and reception after ladies, so will Jeff."

Ben stopped by with his parents.

"Congratulations, Audra, from our whole family," Ben's dad said after they all shook hands.

"And from my mom and me," Audra paused and smiled into Ben's blue eyes, "Ben, congratulations to you."

After Ben's folks drifted to other guests, Ben took Audra aside.

"I wanted you to know this, Audra, I love you. But you and me, we have so many guys and ladies to meet in the next few years. What I'm saying is that we need to date lots of other people, starting now. High school's over, and we've got so much living to do, like your Kids Choir sang, "We've Only Just Begun…to live…"

Audra touched his cheek as they stood outside in a quiet area of the covered patio.

"May I still keep in touch with you through our first year, to see how we're getting along?"

"'Course, I want that, especially see how it's going by Christmas. I'll share this with you. I don't want to upset my folks right now. I'll give Notre Dame everything I've got; I just don't like the feel of the place, so steeped in tradition. I'm not my folks, yeah, you know they're Notre Dame alums.

But, if it isn't going well for me, I'm gonna transfer to the University of Georgia. Notre Dame, well it's pricey, and I think I can get what I need at Georgia, plus I'll have the HOPE, a huge help with tuition."

"I'll not say a word, Ben, you know what you want to do. Maybe at UGA you can do something in drama, or some other interest."

"You blow me away, Audra, always remembering what I really love to do. You've been such a loyal fan of my interests, for a long time now."

"I hope I'll see you sometime this summer."

They hugged and then he led her back into the crowded Davisson home.

He squeezed her hand, "Absolutely, we'll see each other."

&

"You promised, Jeff."

"You're right, Mrs. Tsosie," he smiled and nodded to her and her husband. Audra's other grandparents stood nearby.

The guests left and the group remaining also included Jeff's dad and his mother, and Jeff's sister, Jeannie.

"We want to hear the graduation song again."

Jeff and Audra stood near the piano. Audra played the two notes they needed.

"I'm going to cry, stop it, Audra," she told herself as she continued singing the graduation song with Jeff.

Applause and comments of "wonderful" came from the entire group after they finished the song. The Alicot family said their goodbyes to Audra and her family. Later that afternoon Audra and her mom cooked lots of pizza for the four grandparents. Everyone went to bed early that evening, exhausted from traveling and the graduation day events. The Davisson's returned to Montgomery, leaving early the next morning as they always did. Ashley spent a part of that day with her parents, showing them the law firm office and letting them know what her latest projects were. Later in the afternoon Audra joined them for a hike on the family's favorite trail. They gathered for dinner out, a treat from the Tsosie grandparents to Audra and her mom.

Afterward Audra did a concert: piano, voice, her violin, clarinet, and French horn. They clapped and cheered for her.

"Our granddaughter, a musician and someday music educator," Granddad Tsosie pronounced.

They clapped and cheered again. Everyone sat around the kitchen island and ate graduation cake and drank decaf coffee. The next morning mom and daughter saw her parents off to Atlanta and the long flight back to Helena.

"I got it, Mom. You need to play catch up at work. I'll do the laundry and housework. It was absolutely spectacular to have all my grandparents here."

Several hours later Audra completed her chores. She made the guest beds with the fresh clean sheets. As she flew down the steps to the kitchen, she heard the doorbell ring.

"Jeff, hey, I didn't expect to see you. Come in, your grandma, has she left?"

"Yeah, she rode with Jeannie, back to Atlanta. They both had flights to catch. I've got the house key you gave me. I'm returning it."

"So it's just you and your dad?"

"Yeah, tons of stuff's been happening. I'm working at the city golf course, starting tomorrow."

He walked next to her to the kitchen. She smelled it. And she tried to step back away from him. He grabbed her.

"Cut it out, Jeff, you're holding on to me too tight. What's the matter with you?"

"Babe, I want you, always wanted you, I love you, I want you. I'm gonna have you."

He started to back her against the refrigerator.

"Stop it Jeff, I'm saying no, get away, stop it; you've been drinking."

He held her shoulders against the front of the refrigerator and kissed her hard, his teeth imprinting on her top lip. She felt the bleeding start on her lip and dribble down on his lips. With all her might she kneed him. That broke him away from her. Then she hit him in the face as hard as she could with her fist. He went crashing down on the kitchen floor.

Audra burst into tears as she watched him start to get up. Her mind whirled, "All the times of my life that Jeff's been a part of," she began to cry out, "Jeff, oh my Lord, Jeff."

"Can I sit down?"

"Yes, and I want you to drink two cups of coffee, straight down, do it now."

Audra watched him down the coffee, almost retching before he finished the second cup. Audra sat down in a chair a little away from him. She felt her rapid breathing slow down a little as her right hand began smarting from the punch.

"I'm sorry, Audra, that shouldn't have happened. I came over to return the key you gave me when I stayed with you and Saila. I've kept forgetting. At the last second before I left home, I drank down two shots of rum. That was a horrible mistake. My penis, my hormones, got the best of me. I lost my good sense, and my mind, for a little bit. And with you, my best friend, the person who knows me better'n anybody."

Jeff saw Audra's face, sweaty and teary, her eyes, the corneas completely black. He could feel her anger in her arched shoulders and erect posture. And he couldn't believe how strong she was. His whole groin area ached, and he suspected his eye would blacken. Her punch packed a wallop.

"I feel I'm in a nightmare right now. And I am so," she paused as her tears came, "so disappointed in you. Jeff, you and me, we've talked. You know that my first time, to have sex, will be with a man that I've known for awhile, that I trust, that I care about, and that I love with my whole heart, maybe the man who will be the father of my children someday." He watched her shake her head, "I haven't met that man yet."

"I'd never take that first time away from you, Audra. It's booze talking, wanted to become one with you. I need to get my butt to Alanon, 'cause I could soon have a problem, the booze for my parents, I can't have that fogging my mind."

"I think that's a good idea, Jeff. There's still graduation cake, a few pieces left. I want you to have two pieces of cake. I'll have a piece with you. And I'm making more coffee. You gotta drink two more cups as you eat cake. I won't send you out of my home, until you get a little sobered up. After that, if you get picked up, it's on you; you'll have to live with the consequences."

They ate in silence. Audra looked out at the grand piano. A flood of musical memories came to her, she and Jeff with the a cappella group, for all of those years. She started to tear up again.

"Audra, I love you and I am so sorry."

"I have to let you go now, Jeff, from my life," she nodded as she looked over his head, not into his eyes.

He finished his cake and drank down the second cup of coffee. He excused himself to the bathroom. When he returned he saw that Audra put a covered ice cube on her upper lip. It was just a little before that he noticed the bruised cut, that he had caused.

"In my life, Audra," he gave her eye contact as he spoke, "you've been my precious, my precious one."

He watched the tears slide down her cheeks as she nodded slowly to him.

He put the key on the counter and took his cup, plate and silverware to the sink. He wanted to take her and hold her in his arms. But he walked past her as she sat, back erect and eyes facing forward. He locked the door from the inside and let himself out of the home. He found his car three houses down the street and drove away in a flood of tears.

"My dear God, oh God, I was told, how many times over, to start letting go of Jeff. I am sorry, God, that it ended this way, but I guess it had to, it's Your plan. What I do now is pray for him, as I always have, pray that he has a good life, that he finds his way, whatever that is. And that he finds some happiness, like I'm so happy about my future, all the melodies of my life. Thank you, God, for helping me clear my path, in what I think I want to do."

She sat for a little while longer at the kitchen chair. Her tears started as she cleaned up the dishes they used. She poured coffee, but it hurt her lip to drink it.

That night she shared what happened with her mom. Ashley did not say a word to her daughter; she simply hugged her and told her she loved her.

℘

A week later she had a date with Ben. After the movie they sat in Audra's favorite little café, next door to where her mom ran her campaign for the legislature. She cried and shared what happened to her. Ben wanted to know why she had the greenish bruise and a healing scab on her upper lip.

"I'm so sorry, Audra. You two, always had such a level of trust, like brother and sister. But time's changed all that. What's your plan with him?"

"Like I told God, I pray for Jeff, and his dad, just like I pray for my dad, and my mom. And God knows I pray for you, Ben." She paused and looked into his eyes, "You got lots of decisions to make this next year. And Jeff, well, I've let him go. I do not plan to communicate with him; I'm giving myself at least a year, to get used to him not being in my life."

"You two been friends, how long?"

"Third grade, some wonderful memories, the two of us."

"Keep those good memories, like I'm keeping my good memories of you, Audra.

"Same of me, my tall wonderful knight."

"My beautiful angel."

5

Christmas 2009 – Sophomore Year at Auburn

Audra shivered in the biting cold of that December night. She hurried into her church. She watched the choir members assemble in their places to the back and above the church altar. The technical helper stood to the side, assembling the sound equipment the church choir used for their performances. They quieted as Audra set out the music in sequential order on the music stand the vocal leader used.

"Hey," one of the singers spoke out, "where's Mr. A.?"

Audra moved her eyes from left to right. She held her arms out and shrugged her shoulders and shook her head, giving the group a wide-eyed look of not knowing. Laughter erupted from the group. Audra liked them all, a light-hearted choir who loved to sing. She stood in as leader before.

"Mr. Anderson had two commitments tonight. So he asked me to sub in. You all, I'm headed home tomorrow. I won't be singing with you over the holidays. But I'll be back next year."

"Thank you, Audra for being a part of us," came from a baritone in the top row.

The group clapped and she heard "Yay Audra." She gave them a dramatic bow. Then she lifted her music stick, and they sang. Audra added her maturing alto voice to the endearing Christmas sounds.

The choir and their songs stayed in her head as she drove home to Ephrine. The long drive helped her sort out her past semesters.

"I love my studies," was the stock answer she gave for her experiences at Auburn.

She thought back on the three semesters she accomplished. Brass Instrument Skills, playing her French horn, and learning the other instruments was a bit of challenge for last semester. But she never forgot how hard she had to work spring term of her freshman year, mastering the violin and learning the other string instruments. Everything else paled in comparison to how difficult that class was.

She recalled talking to her mom after her first semester about how she wanted to handle her time with studying and practicing.

"Mom, living in the dorm, that's what I'm gonna do until spring of my senior year, my internship. I don't have time to cook, and it's easy to keep just one room clean in the dorm. I'm not in my room except to eat, go to bed and shower mornings. Otherwise I'm in class or practicing piano, voice or an instrument somewhere on campus. And I'm involved with the Auburn community, singing in a community church choir, just like I'll do when I'm out in the community as a music educator somewhere. I miss my Kids Choir. That's why I'll enjoy spring semester. I'll get to help out with a community children's production, plus they want me for French horn in the orchestra that'll be a part of that spring play."

Her mind swung back to her task at hand. She let herself into her home with her key. She sat her backpack, instrument cases, and bags down near the staircase and walked over to the tree. Her mom told her the tree would be different this year. She plugged in the lights and stood back.

"Wow, this is so bright, the beautiful wide red ribbon she's draped from the top of the tree down to the low branches, nice, Mom," Audra nodded her head, "and multicolored lights, so cheerful."

She went straight to the kitchen and made a big pot of coffee.

"Thanks, Mom, for remembering," she said as she unwrapped the cookies sitting on the kitchen island. She let the taste of oatmeal raisin cookie roll around in her mouth as she took a sip of her coffee.

"I wonder if mom'll get a house sitter, bein' gone for three months?"

She asked herself that as she trudged up the steps with her gear. After she unpacked and changed into her favorite Auburn sweatshirt, she set aside her Christmas present for her mom. It was something her mom asked for when she visited Audra at Thanksgiving in Auburn.

"Gotta wrap it."

She found the wrapping stuff in the guest bedroom closet, where it always was kept. She hummed "Mary's Boy Child," a favorite carol of hers, one that her church choir would do for the holidays.

"I won't be there, 'cept in spirit, guys," she said, thinking of the Auburn adult choir while she wrapped the present.

As her mom walked in later that afternoon she heard Audra tapping on the kitchen island counter. She moved closer and saw her daughter with a wooden spoon in each hand. Ashley heard soft, very fast tapping, then slower and slower louder tapping. Audra moved the spoons off the counter and continued to tap in the air, dancing around and humming to her mom. She stopped, smiled to her mom and then hugged her, spoons still in her hands.

"Hey Mom, I'm starting to work on my percussion, that's my big deal skills for the coming semester."

"Will that be fun?"

"Super awesome, I think, not like the semester of strings."

"Audra."

"Uh, I see that look, Mom, whassup?"

"We're going out to dinner tonight. It's a haf to."

"OK by me, who and where?"

"The Alicot home."

"Oh no," Audra sat down hard on a chair at the kitchen island. She set the spoons down, "Talk to me, Mom."

Ashley watched her daughter's eyes turn jet black.

"It's a long overdue thank you meal, from Sam and Jeff, for everything we did while Sam got help at rehab and Jeff stayed with us, and then graduation. It's also a congratulatory meal, for me, for my new term in the House of Representatives. Actually, Audra," Ashley touched her daughter's arm, "Sam and I have a movie night, every couple of weeks, at either my home, or his, with pizza."

Audra looked into her mom's so dark eyes, "When had you planned on telling me?"

"I just did."

Ashley watched her daughter's eyebrows raise and her forehead furrow.

"I'm reading your mind, dear daughter, yes I know what I am doing. We're good company for each other. We've each lost a spouse, and we have a comfortable relationship together."

As Audra brushed her hair after her shower, her mind continued to blast out spurts of "God, I pray for my mom, and God, please help make my mom happy."

Ashley drove to the Alicot home. Audra felt like she should ask.

"Quick update on Jeff, I've not seen him since graduation. Remember last Christmas we spent time with Grandpa Clint, Grandma Brenda, Madalyn and Abby in Montgomery."

"Yeah, I know, you haven't asked. You strong enough to see him again, Audra?"

"I am," she paused, "older, wiser," she gave her mom a side-wise look and smiled.

Sam greeted them at the front door. Audra watched as he and her mom kissed. Tears burst into Audra's eyes at the shock of seeing that. He hugged Audra, took their coats and hung them in the front closet. Ashley set the bottle of sparkling cider on the kitchen island. Audra looked around at the lovely multicolored lights on the Christmas tree, near the piano in the Alicot great room. She took in a deep breath and inhaled the evergreen smell. And she smelled something else, barbecue. She wiped her tears.

Just then a tall, broad-shouldered man stepped in from the back porch with a plate of cooked steaks in his right hand. He set the steaks down, came to Ashley and kissed her cheek. He moved toward Audra. She stepped back, a little in shock.

"Jeff?"

He smiled as he nodded his head to her.

"She's still my gorgeous precious one," he thought as he continued to smile.

Audra looked him up and down, her mind spinning, "He's grown, I bet three more inches and 25 pounds, hair, so short, can't hardly see the color, he's buffed, look at those shoulders."

"May I hug you, Audra?"

"I," she paused as she looked up to him, "I guess so."

They came together in a quiet hug and let go quickly. In the background Audra could see her mom and Jeff's dad looking at them.

"Soup's on, everyone. Ashley, please pour the cider."

They sat down and consumed lots of salad, steak, baked potatoes, and rolls.

"I can't believe how hungry I am," Audra thought as she dug into a second small piece of medium-well-done steak.

The parents carried the conversation, until after everyone helped clean up the dishes. Decaf coffee went all around to the group as they sat in the great room, Audra and Ashley on the couch and Jeff and Sam in comfortable chairs opposite them. Everyone wanted to wait for dessert, chocolate or carrot cake.

Ashley looked at her daughter with her lawyer's start-talking gaze.

"Jeff," Audra directed her eyes to him, "we haven't talked since high school graduation, fill me in."

"Sure, this is old news for your mom and my dad, but I'm at UGA now, second semester, and I see your eyes asking, I have the HOPE. I'm doing so good. The best thing I did was taking last year away from studying, workin' my butt off, the old golf course, real slave labor. But I'll go back in the summer, unless I get something more lucrative. And I'm happy with my major, accounting, gonna try for the CPA which means I gotta have a masters."

"Wow, Jeff, that's so great," she smiled to him as she spoke in a happy voice.

"Now you, Audra, I just know a little, from your mom," Jeff smiled to Ashley.

"Music education is wild, so many parts, the vocal, the piano, all the instruments in an orchestra and in a band, plus I volunteer, am in a church choir, and help out with community theater productions at an Auburn nonprofit. This coming semester I have percussion skills, get to learn the drums, snare, bass, tympani. I got a class in school and community general music education. I imagine I for sure will be at a school, or some kind of community music, remember me having Senior Sing and Kids Choir?"

"I won't forget those high school times, Audra," he nodded to her.

"Gonna be bold, 'cause I'll share, I hope you've met ladies at UGA."

"I have, lots of women in my accounting classes, unbelievable. I've met a sophomore I really like, transfer from."

He looked at Audra.

"Auburn?"

"Right, back in Georgia, like me, she's got HOPE too."

"I'm seeing two different fellas, and they're totally as opposite as they can be, a junior music education major, uber talented, and a guy in Auburn's School of Veterinary

Medicine, he's third year, older. Both these guys are like me, so busy. I see them on an occasional basis."

Sam interjected, "Audra, you have so many commitments, in so many directions."

"She certainly does have, and Dad, just the opposite for me, I'm more concentrated, just classrooms and the library, basically."

Just then Audra wanted so much to ask Jeff to hop up and join her in one of the old songs they did as part of a cappella. But she just decided it would be too painful when they finished the song. She had, in slow fashion, begun to release her memories of Jeff.

They got cake and took it back to where they were sitting. Sam lit the gas fireplace. Audra watched the fire and ate, feeling a warmth, a coziness she had not experienced for some time. It was being with her mom, and what really surprised her, with Jeff.

&

Audra breathed in the cool mountain air. A breeze touched her cheeks. She turned and smiled to Ben.

"The best, hiking, especially with a cool dude."

He touched her shoulder as they descended the mountain, "Especially with my angel."

She looked back to see her mom and Sam, hand in hand, taking the hike down slower than she and Ben did. Audra's mom promised them an early dinner out, at a place of Ben and Audra's choosing. They chose Italian, and, of course, pizza, Audra, pepperoni, and Ben, hamburger, with extra cheese.

They sat in the busy restaurant, enjoying their pop and favorite pizza.

"Dr. Alicot?"

"Just Sam, OK Ben?"

"OK," he paused and smiled to Sam, "My HOPE is really helping; easing my money situation, but I have catch up, 'cause when I left Notre Dame, I just took care of my core stuff there. I'm finding my initial accounting classes to be a challenge."

"The deal is, Ben, accounting takes a huge amount of time, the problems, just lots of time. You've got to make a commitment of that time and energy, to stick it out. Later on you'll find aspects of accounting you'll like better, like auditing, or cost accounting, or, like me, tax accounting."

"That's what you teach at Humphrey, tax accounting?"

"Right, plus the first accounting class students take. Many majors need the basic accounting class."

"You have help?"

"I do, with all the homework students have, I keep three grad students busy, all semester long. Just hang in there, Ben, you need time, and time management."

"Like you have to do, Audra, with your commitments off and on campus."

"Sometimes there aren't enough hours in the day."

Ben nodded his head to all of them, "OK, got it, manage my time, glad I'm not working a part time gig of any kind. And the thought of drama, the stage, I've had to let go of that."

"I'd say you're out in the real world now," Ashley smiled to Ben.

"Right."

Ben took Audra home in his car. She invited him in for decaf coffee and conversation at the big kitchen island.

"I have a nice friend, Audra, she reminds me a little of you, also in accounting. She's a junior so can talk to me about what's coming up in my course work."

"I see a little bit of two guys, a so super talented guy in our music education program, a junior, and a third year student in the vet med program. He's mid-twenties, and he'll be a fine veterinarian, a motivated, on-fire kind. He's a big guy, and he wants to work with large animals besides little, the two dudes, so completely different from each other."

"Hey, they like you, the one guy, 'cause you two are comfortable together, with the same major, you speak the same language. And the vet student, he likes you because you're exotic, way opposite of anyone that he's around all day."

"I've never had a dog or a cat, not even a goldfish. But he seems to understand, that I live in a world of melodies, of music. He lives in a world of animals. He's invited me to the School of Veterinary Medicine Open House for the whole Auburn community. That comes up half way through the semester."

"The girl I like, she's quiet, I'm finding out, kinda typical accounting type. I have to draw her out to get her to talk. She's going straight on for her masters, so she can get her CPA."

"A masters for a CPA?"

"Yeah, that's the rule, at least in the state of Georgia, can't sit for the CPA unless you've got the masters."

"Wow."

"Wow is right, accounting, with all the different divisions, and different rules, laws, etc. you gotta have so much knowledge."

He stopped talking and looked to her, smiling.

"Duh, that's no different than all the instruments you've learned, all the different aspects of music, oh my goodness, Audra, there is so much to learn, no matter what field a person's in."

"For sure."

"It's been good to see you, New Year's plans?"

"Uh huh, we'll be in Montgomery with Grandpa Clint and Grandma Brenda."

"Will Abby be there?"

"Nope, hey she's loving her nursing program, did I hear you say something at dinner about getting to know her better?"

"You did, I met her with you last summer. My heart did a little flip flop."

"Yeah, that happens to lots of folks; we look so much alike," she nodded, "it's dad."

"Unbelievable."

"Yeah, people say that also."

Audra smiled and giggled to him.

Ashley came home and joined them in the kitchen.

"It was fun, the hike, and thanks again for the pizza, Ashley, good luck with your legislative session."

"Thanks, it'll be hoppin'."

"Gotta head home."

"I'll walk you out."

Audra got his coat and helped him on with it.

They stood on the front porch and hugged.

"Happy New Year, Audra."

"And Happy New Year to you, dear Ben."

"Study hard, God bless you."

"And God bless and keep you."

He kissed her on top of her head and let go of her hand. She stood and watched him walk to his car. He turned and waved to her before he got in. She smiled and waved back.

ॐ

Audra moved among the guests at her grandparents' New Year's Eve potluck. Folks in the Davisson neighborhood enjoyed staying home on this special night. This year the Davisson's hosted the potluck. Ashley greeted guests at the front door. Clint and Brenda took food from the guests and set it out on the wide kitchen island. Guests put their coats in Clint's nearby study. Everyone headed for the big open kitchen and helped themselves to decaf coffee, pop, beer, and wine.

Audra turned from talking to a guest and caught his eye. He turned from talking to her mom. She saw his friendly smile.

She walked to him, as he moved to her, giving him her wide smile, "Oh, Austin, I'm so glad you're able to come. I didn't know when you'd get off your shift at the hospital."

"Missy, I wouldn't miss this time with you. I got somebody to cover for me for a few hours, gotta drive back, be there at midnight."

They hugged. Audra felt his strength in his wide shoulders and long arms. He felt her tall small frame as they stayed in their hug for several moments.

A flash of light passed through his mind.

"She's the one, God, she is."

They let go of each other. Audra guided him to the coffee pot. Like her, he drank lots of coffee, and Audra remembered. They moved to a quiet corner of the Davisson living room with coffee in hand.

"Audra, something just happened, in my head. You've told me in the past that your dad always called you his bright light. Is that accurate?"

"All my life, he said, from the time I was born, that's what he said of me."

"This's gonna sound crazy, but while we were hugging, a bright light flashed through my head."

"Yeah, that's what dad always saw, what he told me, that's why he called me his bright light."

"Incredible."

He saw the somber look on Audra's face, unsmiling.

"Oooh, that brings up her dad; I think she's had a hard time letting him go," he thought.

Audra took him to her grandparents and introduced them to him. They chatted, interested in his plans for his future. Ashley signaled her daughter as Audra walked away from her grandparents and Austin.

"Dra, please, the crew is getting hungry and your grandma asked that you say grace."

After a couple of minutes Ashley got the group's attention and announced the grace message.

Audra spoke up with her strong voice, "This is from Ralph Waldo Emerson, be thankful, for each new morning with its light, for rest and shelter of the night, for health and food, for love and friends, for everything THY goodness sends."

Everyone joined in, "Amen."

Audra and Austin sat on stools close to the lit fireplace. They balanced their plates of food on their knees.

"I love surgery. I want to do some work on horses' knees, like repairing damage."

"How?"

"In the summer, I'll be in a clinical rotation, two surgeons in the program who do awesome work, bringing back horses that, well, under usual circumstances, would be put down."

"So, they're super valuable horses?"

"Yeah, like the equestrian, race, and show horses."

"Wow, I've heard and read of vets, uh, like rehab horses who go on to race in the big races, like the Kentucky Derby, the Preakness."

"That's right, you know how athletes have ACL and MCL surgery to repair knees, procedures like that, with horses."

"Ready for another plate?"

They got up together and went back for second helpings.

"More coffee?" he asked her as they started to sit back down.

"Yes, thanks," Audra nodded to him.

After they started in on the food, Audra remembered something he said.

"You mentioned this summer, are you in school?"

"Absolutely, from the summer through fall and spring semesters, all of us finishing vet students have 24 2-week rotations we have to work into our schedules in order to graduate, 15 required rotations and 9 elective. Then, a year from April, when I've got my DVM, I'll be taking the NAVLE, that's the exam of the National Board of Vet Medicine examiners."

"Gotta be licensed?"

"'Course, can't practice without that. Plus Alabama also has its own Vet exam, kinda at the same time at the National Board Exam. Until then I'll just be working as a kind of advanced vet tech somewhere in Alabama, deciding where I want to practice."

"So I'll be certified, to teach in Alabama, provided I got all the classes certification requires, which I will have and of course, my degree."

"There's lots more required, Audra, than just graduating with a particular degree."

"I guess I always knew that, just didn't realize what a big deal it was, going through the process."

She looked into his hazel eyes, tonight picking up a greenish light.

"We got a lot ahead of us. And I'll grab dessert now with you, and be headed back to Auburn. My little job'll be over as soon as classes start up again. But it's been great to be behind the scenes watching and helping the animals to heal before we send them back to their owners."

"I'm so happy you came, to meet my grandparents and to see mom again."

"Wouldn't have missed it; we'll find time to be together, and, you've gotta come to the Open House mid semester, uh, I mean, I'd really like you to see what we do."

"It's already on my calendar; it sounds so fun, with little children bringing their stuffed animals to be stitched up, pretend broken bones fixed up, and to see a simple surgery or two, on real live animals, oh and how you care for the sick and injured animals."

She emphasized real and live, and he laughed with her, "Yeah, it's awesome, Auburn, the community's not that large, but I'll tell you from the past two years, the crowds who visit us, they're friendly and fun, and they really enjoy the tour by the vet students."

They each chose Black Forest Cake for their dessert.

"Chocoholic," Audra nodded, "uuummmm."

"Yeah, also for me, sometimes I even have chocolate cereal for breakfast."

"Here's a to-go cup with lid, coffee inside, you gotta stay awake on that drive back. You know what the roads are gonna be like."

"Thanks, Audra, yeah I do know. I'll be careful."

She helped him find his coat in her grandpa's study. He set his coffee down.

"Audra?"

He stepped to her and encircled her with his arms. She put her arms around his back and held him.

"Yes?"

They looked into each other's eyes.

"I'm in love with you. And I want to be with you, when we can be. I got so much ahead, and so do you, Missy."

They stepped back from each other.

Audra nodded, a mist in her eyes, "And I am in love with you, have been since I saw you, in your flapping white coat, so much the doctor, as I brought in the little dog that'd been hit and left for dead on the road. The way you strode over to me, so much in control, so concerned about the little animal."

"I remember it well; you'd been crying so hard, that a human had just driven away, without any regard for life."

They smiled to each other.

"You be safe out there; we've got so much living to do, Austin."

"Happy New Year, Audra."

"And Happy New Year to you."

He gave her a soft kiss and she kissed him back. Then he kissed her on top of her head.

"These kisses from him," she thought, "this night I'll remember."

&

Audra waved to him as he raised his eyes to the audience watching him help with the spaying of the little dog. She saw him give her a tiny nod.

"He sees me, nice."

Later during the Vet Med Open House he found her as she stepped away from a short lecture on animal nutrition.

"Austin."

He grooved on the way she smiled to him, her dark eyes lighting up, warming to him.

"I saw you."

"Yeah, I could tell you did."

"I'm so glad I came. It's fun to see the little beasts get well."

"Caution," she watched his hazel eyes darken to almost brown, "we don't save every beast or bird."

"I know that, what I can't believe is the number of cancers that you docs find in all kinds of animals. Have the cancers always been there?"

They found their way to the refreshment area.

"Yes, it's taken lots of technology to discover exactly what's bothering animals. Lab work, Cat Scans, MRI's, those abilities have helped vet docs so much in the last 20 years."

ℂ

Grandpa Clint and Grandma Brenda wanted to give Audra her graduation present early. They also talked to Madalyn. Abby was their granddaughter too.

The summer before the girls' senior year at Auburn, the four of them embarked on a 15-day cruise.

"Ladies," Clint spoke up as they made their final plans, "we're gonna let you and friends do Ireland, England, and France one day on your own. What we'll do is rivers, the Rhine and Danube, on a smaller cruise line, with fewer guests, more intimate."

"What countries?" Abby asked.

"We've decided to spend that 15 days in the Netherlands, Germany, Austria, and Hungary."

"Oh my gosh, my first trip to Europe," Abby smiled, grabbing Grandma Brenda's hand.

"And mine, so awesome," Audra nodded, "and doing it in such a pleasant way."

"We'll be off the boat a lot for trips into the cities we'll be passing by."

℘

One evening after they came back to the cruiser from a concert in a town Audra and Abby had a chance to talk in the bedroom they shared. They sat across from each other, on their twin beds.

"How blessed are we to have grandparents like Grandpa Clint and Grandma Brenda."

"Yeah, and Abby, we've told them so. They groove on the little appreciations we share with them. And, for sure, this is the time when we could do this trip, next summer," she stopped.

"Uh huh, next summer we're looking for work; I'm taking my RN boards."

"And I hope I'll have narrowed my search for the music education job I want, or have gotten it."

"Audra, Ben wants to date me."

She paused, deciding what she wanted to say, "Really, good for you, Abby," she gave her sister a wide smile, and Abby heard the happiness in Audra's voice.

"Gosh," Audra thought a moment before she went one, "that'll be tough with you two in different states, and him with so much of his program left to go. He's awesome."

Audra remembered then, a conversation she had with Ben, at the graduation party for Jeff and her, those three years back.

"Need to share, Ben and I stood out on our back patio, the afternoon after our morning graduation from Ephrine High. We went to prom together, and he seemed unclear if Notre Dame was the correct school for him. Anyway, I'm getting away from my point."

"Go ahead, Audra."

"On the patio we stood and talked about dating and what changes our lives were making 'cause we were headed for college. He wanted to date other girls, and he expressed that to me. I heard the maturity in his thinking when he mentioned all the people we would date as we moved on with our lives. And so he wanted me to date other guys, especially at Auburn."

"We love, Audra."

"Yeah, we love, each other, our families, and we continue to add to our capacity to love, with all the people we're meeting along the way, you in nursing, and me, in the whole world of music, so many people, so much caring."

"It's love building on love."

"Yeah, reason why God put us on this earth," Audra nodded, smiling to Abby. "And I'm thinking of our dad."

"Uh huh, like you've always said, up there riding along on the clouds."

∛

Spring 2012 Audra settled into her internship, at Sanburn Overt High School in Montgomery, Alabama. She chose the school, and her internship coordinator at Auburn found the Overt High music instructor willing to take on a student intern for a semester. Audra liked what she saw going on at this school. Many students found an interest in music, art, drama, and there was a big poetry society. The school's namesake was a long-ago poet known in that area of the South.

The students wore uniforms. The 9th graders wore a different color collared polo shirt from the upper class sophomores, junior, and seniors. Tan had to be the color of students' skirts or pants. Audra liked that because the students seemed to act better, taking more pride in the way they looked and responded to their school. Overt High came to be in the early 1900's, lots of renovations over the years as Audra could see. The school's exterior still looked the same as it had in the early days. To Audra it felt more like a small private college campus.

She got used to visitors in her classrooms. Today, in the band room, the high school principal stopped in to say hello and listen to the band. Once they finished the piece the principal applauded.

"Now, let me hear something, well," he paused and smiled to them, "livelier."

Audra gazed around. She acknowledged the upraised hand.

"Miss D., the one?"

Audra nodded. They began the rock song, ratcheted the noise level up a bit, and every band member moved to the beat of the music. Audra stepped away from the front of the band, moving from side to side and clapping her hands. The principal came to her.

"Dance?"

She smiled up to him and nodded. He whirled and twirled her in the front of the band room as they continued to play. The song ended, and the whole band clapped and cheered for Miss D. and Mr. Klawson. He remembered reading her internship application, that she possessed long-time dancing and drama skills, in addition to music and vocal. The two dancers bowed to each other. Cheers erupted from the band.

And that's how the story got told, that day the principal danced for the band, oh, and with the band director, no less.

℃

Audra's mentor at Overt High, Mrs. Gillingham, allowed Audra to take over all the classes that Mrs. Gillingham taught. This was one week after Audra began her internship. That meant two days a week Audra spent two hours at a nearby elementary school, working with 4th and 5th graders. They exuded wonderful talent. In some ways they reminded her of her Kids Choir back in Ephrine. What it meant for Mrs. Gillingham was she got to assist with a special project with which the principal was tasked. She absolutely had that level of trust for Audra working with her students, no matter if they were in band, or orchestra, or wind ensemble, or chorus, or glee. Another instructor worked with drama and pep band students.

And then the drama instructor got in an automobile accident. She had serious leg injuries. The school administration talked to Audra, knowing about her extensive previous drama experience, both as an actor, and dancer, but also in filling in for the injured play director in one of Auburn's Community Theater productions. Her internship coordinator from Auburn happened to be on site that day. Mrs. McCallum sat down with Audra and Mr. Klawson at the conference table in his office.

"Mrs. Gillingham's covering for you at the elementary school, so we can talk to you, Audra. You know our drama teacher is out, probably for the rest of the semester."

"I heard, and I am so sorry. Tell me what I can do to help out."

"Would you be willing to take on the drama production, planned for early April?"

"What play?"

"*Arsenic and Old Lace.*"

"Yes, of course, I can do that. My high school produced it one year. I was Elaine."

Audra noticed the blank looks on their faces.

"Uh, Elaine, she was a main character, in love with Mortimer, the other main character in *Arsenic.*"

Audra smiled to them both, "What a fun and super crazy play it was. We had such a great time doing it."

She saw the now serious look on the principal's face, not light-hearted as she observed when he was in the band room.

"Concerns, Mr. Klawson?"

"It hasn't been cast yet. And it's the second week in February. You'd have eight weeks to get ready."

"So early April, yes, this is very doable. But that will mean practices, early evening?"

"Right, four nights a week, Monday through Thursday, some weeks only three nights because these students have so many other commitments, but really like the drama, uh and we'll lose spring break week, that's close to the play time."

"Well, we'll be OK, not to worry folks, there is so much talent at this school, the students and their writing, poetry, the music some of them compose, rap, and classical, the glee club. Oh my gosh, my head spins when I think of how musical many of them are."

℘

"He can come, oh, my, gosh, he can come."

Audra grabbed her grandma and hugged her.

"Please, please, Dra, who can come? Sit down and tell me."

"Saturday night, last performance of *Arsenic*, Austin can get away and drive here. Can we put him up?"

"Your mom'll be here, right?"

"Uh huh, she's driving in from Atlanta, she's got final wrap up of all the legislative stuff from this term."

"Certainly, we got two more spare bedrooms, so everyone'll get their own room."

"Thanks, Grandma, and I am telling you again how much I appreciate being able to stay with you and grandpa while I'm doing my internship at Overt High."

"We've certainly enjoyed having you, Audra. You light up our home, and us also, with all your musical sounds, it's a liveliness we'll always cherish."

"Thanks, Grandma Brenda, you've been here lots more than Grandpa Clint."

"It's been my great pleasure, to have you here in my life, Audra."

They hugged again.

Audra danced up the stairs to her room.

"To see Austin, again," she sang out.

She sat on her bed, and put the music she worked on aside. She thought about him, "I got to see him, at his graduation, a doctor, oh my goodness. And I met his pops and momma, that's what he calls them, and his sister, Ali, a nurse in Birmingham. I think they liked me OK, but I'm totally different from anyone in Austin's whole family. They're all soft spoken, like Austin, and I, well, I'm musical, kinda noisy, doin' what I love. Then I saw him briefly before Christmas, as I finished my last final for that semester, my final semester on the Auburn campus."

In e-mails from him since then she learned he changed locations from way down south by Mobile and worked now as a fill-in vet tech near Florence, in the north west part of the state. He sent short messages. She remembered all the previous months, late nights and early mornings he studied for his exams coming up later in the month.

"He's taking a break, coming to see me. He must be ready, for the tests, kinda like I was before my auditions for the Auburn ME program."

She shared that with her grandparents that Friday evening at dinner.

"One more week, right Audra?"

She nodded to her Grandpa Clint, "Two practices, dress rehearsal Wednesday, and three nights of the play, Thursday through Saturday."

"And we're all coming Saturday night, right?"

She smiled and nodded to them.

℘

"Watch for it, watch for it," he remembered Audra telling him about the scene she added to this production of *Arsenic*. It was a very small addition, a scene she and Ben created back at Ephrine High. Audra shared that her main characters in this production, Elaine, and Mortimer, really like doing the scene, just as she and Ben did.

"Wow, the two of them sang and danced, and then, singing a marriage proposal. It was," he paused, "romantic, " Austin shared with Ashley at the break before the next act.

"Audra let you know how super talented the kids at this school are," Ashley said.

"I had no idea. I can hardly dance a lick, but these kids, they seem very professional, the dancing, and the acting."

"And they can sing, oh my gosh," Grandma Brenda turned to share with Austin and Ashley.

Austin stayed with Audra to help students strike the set. Audra got 8 sets of parents of participants in *Arsenic* to pony up for pizza. She provided pop. Before the cast left each other that night they gathered around Audra to do their cheer for her. That prompted Audra to suggest a quick replay of a scene from the play. The play participants and parents stood around on the stage as a favorite scene got picked. It involved four actors and mayhem going on around them with a character appearing and then disappearing from the stage. Everyone laughed and cheered and said their goodbyes.

"Awesome, Audra, it was so much fun watching you watch them. You do such a great job. I haven't heard your band, orchestra, or glee group."

"They're just as much fun for me, and they have fun together."

They held hands as they walked into the Davisson home. A coffee smell tickled their noses.

Audra set her bags down near the stairs and took their coats.

"It's decaf, Austin, mom left a note."

"Cookies?"

"Course, this is the cookie-eating family."

"Oatmeal raisin?"

They sat next to each other at the kitchen island, drinking coffee and eating the cookies.

"Uh huh, and I know you gotta head out at the crack of dawn, so I'll say it now, you're in my thoughts and prayers, as you take your exams and decide from there."

"Thanks, and Audra, I've narrowed my search down to the northern part of Alabama. They're several older vets who're lookin' to retire within five years, and are wantin' to bring on a young partner, to take over, and buy him out."

"Oh my gosh, one day at a time, right?"

"Uh huh, always, and forever, we're in God's hands."

&

Audra ran a brush through her hair after she tossed on her Auburn sweatshirt. She ran down the steps and started the coffee she set up last night. She found the donuts and set them on the kitchen island.　She felt someone behind her. Austin moved closer and put his arms around her waist.

"Mornin' Missy, how was your sleep, a quick one?"

She turned around and kissed him. He returned her kiss with a longer one of his own. She felt his soft caressing lips against her own.

"I had a hard time getting to sleep, the late pizza, and cookies, and thinking of you."

Ashley joined them, "Early morning, guys," she said as she poured a cup of coffee.

"See, Audra," her mom smiled to her as she turned around.

"You're wearing the Auburn sweatshirt I gave you for Christmas several years ago, nice Mom."

"I wear it a lot, and I really like it, never been much of a sweatshirt person, but this one is warm and comfortable. Hey, you two, I'll head back to bed, but I wanted to say goodbye, Austin, and to thank you for being so considerate, seeing Audra's production."

"I wouldn't 'a missed seeing Audra, and the play."

"Safe travels, Austin, I know you're going to be making some big decisions for your future."

Ashley and Austin hugged. She took her coffee and took steps back up to her room.　After two donuts each and another partial cup of coffee Audra and Austin parted while Austin got ready to leave.

"Missy," he touched her cheek as they stood together near the front door, "I'll try to get here for your graduation."

"Thank you, Austin, for coming. E-mails'll be our life line. I'm applying for music ed jobs in Alabama, from Birmingham north. It'll be a challenge, 'cause some districts lost programs during the really bad days after the financial crises."

"God's watchin' over you, and so am I. You'll find what you're supposed to have."

She watched his hazel eyes with their green shine, his happy eyes. She let out a big breath and nodded her head to him. They hugged.

"Stay in, there's a bit of a chill, felt it on my first trip out to the car this morning."

"I love you, Austin."

"I love you, Audra."

He kissed her on top of her head. Audra opened her grandparents' front door, and he walked out to a view of the just rising sun, a pinky and orange glob. She returned to the kitchen and fixed herself a half cup of coffee. She remembered, church with her grandparents, and seeing her mom off to Atlanta.

෮

"I can't believe it, Grandpa Clint."

He put his arm around her shoulders as they walked away from the ceremony.

"Believe it, Audra, dear, you're graduated. And it looks like, well, you've talked like you're deciding between school districts and their programs up north."

"I am, and I have to let both schools know by a week from yesterday, next Friday."

"Weigh the pros and cons, and the challenges, just remember how difficult it's been for schools since the downturn of the economy back in '08."

Two hours later Audra, Ashley, Grandma Brenda and Grandpa Clint sat with Madalyn and her parents. Abby's small nursing graduation ceremony contrasted to the huge assemblage for Audra's graduation. Audra liked this ceremony so much better, the intimacy of the smaller group.

She teared up as the family took turns hugging Abby after the ceremony. After she hugged Abby and congratulated her, Audra's tears came harder.

Ashley stepped to her daughter, "You OK?"

Audra whispered in her ear, "Dad, Austin, missing them."

Ashley nodded and let Audra have a moment away from the rest of the group.

"Dad, you're here, I feel you next to me. I shouldn't be such a baby," she told herself, "Austin had an emergency at the clinic, and he couldn't get away. But I'm sad he isn't here. He's a doctor, get a grip, Audra, emergencies are a part of his life."

Abby's sorority had an all day celebration for its sisters who graduated. Abby's entire family joined her for cake, fruit and veggie plates, and punch. They sat and ate at a long table in the elegant dining room of the sorority house. Several close sorority sisters, also fellow graduates of Abby's, stopped by to meet her family and to wish Abby well in her future nursing endeavors. Audra enjoyed the happy laughter and joy she saw all around in the room.

"Any other nurses in your sorority graduating class?"

"I'm the only one, Grandma Brenda; they're educators, like Brianne, who Audra knows, business administration, accountants, criminal justice, going on to law school, and several biomedical science majors headed for medical school."

"Uh huh, Brianne's making decisions about where she'll teach," Audra added.

"I've made a decision, guys," Abby announced to her family as they sat together.

"Tell us, dear."

"Going straight on for my Nurse Practitioner, need the masters for that and then much more training. In a few years,

I'll be right along side the docs, writing prescriptions, doing little surgery procedures."

Madalyn nodded her head, "She told me, after she sat for her RN boards."

Everyone clapped and cheered for Abby.

℘

Audra loved Robert Frost's poem about the road less traveled. She chose a smaller school district, on a road less traveled, Riniville, Alabama. Just a few minutes away sat the community of Fort Porter, a much larger town. She felt happy about her choice of a smaller school district rather than the one in Fort Porter, not far off an Interstate in northeast Alabama.

"I'm glad I made up my mind. But I have huge challenges ahead."

The school district just brought back music. Since 2008 there had been music silence in the schools. A long-time music teacher in the community, not affiliated with the schools, wrote a grant, with the assistant principal. He saw a need, for music. The school district got awarded the grant, part of it to help pay for a music education instructor for the schools for the next three years. The school principal and this grant writer sat in on the interviews with Audra and two other applicants for the position. After he listened to the way Audra volunteered in community and church music activities in addition to music in the schools, the grant writer cast the deciding vote to bring her to the Riniville schools.

℘

She and Austin had not e-mailed since she packed her car and headed back to Ephrine after graduation. They talked briefly on their cells. He knew Audra accepted a position in Riniville. In a short e-mail to her, he wrote, "Sheez, I'm still waffling between two different vet practices. Both have many good, but a few not-so-good qualities."

Audra e-mailed him back, "Hey, when I get in my struggles, I always check in with God, pray, and ask for His advice. What I know is that He's in charge, and it's His will for each of us. You had one doc at the vet school that kind of was your mentor. If you haven't already, I'd get his thoughts on what you're thinking of doing. All this's gonna take years, Austin. If we end up anywhere near each other, I sincerely want to help you, your dream, a vet practice. I'm getting my dream, at least for the next few years. Hey, and we don't know each other that well, it will be good for us to see each other more often. Our time over these past years, that we've spent together, scattered."

&

"I've worked in both locations, so why can't I make up my mind about where I want to be?" he stewed about that day after day.

He took Audra's advice and called his mentor at the Vet School. He got his exam results, now a certified DVM in the state of Alabama. One evening he decided to play the DVD Audra sent him of the final production of *Arsenic and Old Lace.* He laughed and cheered and enjoyed the play, more so now that he knew the story and how Audra influenced it.

"She has such a gift, of getting young people to showcase the talent that's in them. And she sure doesn't see color; every single actor and helper in the production at Overt High was black. What she does is plant a seed, and she gets these kids to blossom in great ways," he thought.

His next day off he drove to the vet and his practice near the outskirts of Fort Porter. Dr. Hallad had a little time, so Austin took him out to lunch. They talked, and Austin signed the paperwork to begin the process of taking over the practice, a five-year process. He kept his e-mails cheerful to Audra.

Audra found an apartment, several days after she moved to Riniville. And she started going in to school. It was early

August and her contract hadn't started, but she didn't care. Her first morning the piano and violin music teacher who helped with the grant writing met her at school.

"Once the program closed, the school music educator took the time to show me around the music area. I think he suspected that the whole school administration and most of the teachers would change in the next years, and he told me he thought I might be the only contact, if music ever returned."

Audra smiled to him, "Which it has, and I really appreciate you coming in, and that the school kept this area, like they saved it for a time music would thrive again."

Albert Garner showed her around the music areas, abandoned for these years since the program folded for lack of funds. She felt so happy, because she had so much. Then he took her to the storage areas. Equipment for a small band, for a small orchestra, and so much music, all was stored away by the conscientious teacher who lost his job in '08. Her third morning at school she started checking the condition of all the equipment. The helpful community teacher warned her.

She sat, with her own cherished French horn near her. Audra spent the last two hours bringing out stored away folding chairs and music stands, getting them set up in the band/orchestra area of the room. She pulled up the blinds, bringing light into the room.

"Wow, this is such a bright and cheerful area," she spoke out.

She placed six different instruments in their cases around her. She sat and opened up the clarinet case. Several sections of the clarinet fell out. She felt each piece, checking for damage. Audra heard someone walking toward her in the band room. She turned with a clarinet piece in her hand.

"Missy."

"Oh Austin," she rose up, set the clarinet part down, and went to him, "oh my gosh, it's so good to see you."

They hugged. He kissed her, a soft feathery kiss.

"You're here, to, to?"

He saw her furrowed brow and questioning look.

"Tell you I took on the practice in Fort Porter."

"In Fort Porter," she stopped, her thinking jumbled with the surprise of his coming into her band room, "uh, that's just the next town over. I think I told you I interviewed there."

"Uh huh, but you also told me you decided on a road less traveled, Riniville."

They stood together, surrounded by instruments that lay on the floor for Audra to look over.

He flushed, a bright light flashing through his mind.

"Audra, I love you."

"Austin, I love you," she looked at the happy smile on his face.

"I want to marry you, Audra, to be with you, for the rest of our lives."

Her tears came, and all she could do was nod.

He looked into her tear-filled eyes, "That bright light flashed through my head, a bright light, for my future, for your future."

She saw his nod to her, "Together."

LOVE TIES

Over a hundred years love intertwines four young women. Caring for their Colorado land and loving their men thread through the hope these teens have for their families and their futures.

El meets W.D. as they homestead in northeastern Colorado. Their passionate attraction leads to their marriage with a baby coming six months later. El remains constant in her vow to care for her thriving land. She imparts this caring especially to her granddaughter, Michelle.

Michelle and Brett fall in love while at State University. After he serves in Vietnam and finishes his degree, he and Michelle marry. Oil is discovered on property Brett inherits. They adopt Tessa. As with her grandmother Michelle understand she is but a guardian of the land.

Tessa locates her birth parents, Dawn and Billy. They relate to her the story of their love and reuniting. Tessa now understands the circumstances of her adoption.

Tessa meets Coy at his hospital construction site. They fall in love. Tessa completes her job as site supervisor of a middle school and finishes Coy's hospital construction. They marry. The land on which Tessa and Coy build projects is land fiercely loved by Tessa, Michelle and El. Tessa, Michelle, Dawn, and El tie to each other, their love for their husbands and families.

About Cathleen

www.CathleenEllis.com

Cathleen Ellis is a Colorado native. She and her husband, John, live in the northern part of the state. They have four sons, three daughters-in-law, and four grandchildren. Cathleen draws the inspiration for her love stories from the lives of young people with whom she has lived and worked her entire life.

9 781629 671482